# MAID IN DUBAI

*Zana Bonafe*

Copyright © 2018 Zana Bonafe
All rights reserved.
No part of this book may be used or reproduced in any manner whatsoever without written permission from the author except in the case of brief quotations embodied in critical articles or reviews.
ISBN: 978 17 20423478

This book is dedicated to Lena, Miro, Ahmed and Maya; my endless suppliers of love, inspiration and support.

## ACKNOWLEDGMENTS

I am very grateful to Abigail Stefaniak for her exceptional editing skills, to the talented Jeanly Zamora for her creativity, and to all the expatriates who were open and forthcoming about their experiences abroad.

# PROLOGUE

## THE BEGINNING OF SEASONS

I never meant for this to be a book. At first, it was just a way to kill time on the endless commuting trips from my accommodation to the houses of clients. It may sound arrogant to say 'clients', but nonetheless, they were. Although I was only cleaning their houses, I was providing a service and they paid me for it. In my mind, I was not a maid. I was a service provider.

When I came to Dubai, the one thing no one told me was how long the commuting would take. I saw all the glamour of Dubai on TV and although I did not fool myself into thinking I would be in an opulent house with golden horses at the entrance, I expected to be somewhere central, maybe sharing a room with another girl, in an airy and clean apartment.

My accommodation in Dubai was clean and far larger than my own home back in the Philippines. However, I was sharing the bedroom with five other women, and not all of them were girls my age. Four were married with children, who were now being looked after by their grandmothers in the Philippines. The other bedroom in the house was just as full. And to make matters worse, my apartment was not in Dubai. It was in the neighbouring Emirate, called Sharjah. If one would consider the concept of Dubai as all the buildings and streets that are interconnected, then Sharjah would be considered Greater Dubai and you would not be able to tell where one city ends and the next one begins. But, it was another city, another Emirate... one that on a good day, was only twenty-five minutes away from my employer's head office. On a bad day, you could assume three hours. These notes were written mainly on bad days... which happened quite often.

# SUMMER – 2008

# 1

# DUBAI DESTINY

I have always believed in destiny! I believed that a greater force was always in charge of my life and that all I could do was pray and hold on tight to my sanity as the wild horse of my life would gallop in unforeseen directions.

Destiny brought me to Dubai. I came from a small village in the Juban District, in the south of the most important and largest island of the Philippines: Luzon. It was in Luzon that the capital Manila was situated, as well as the airport I was departing from. Normally, I would not even mention the name of my village because no one knew where it was, not even my friends Maricar and Mariann, who seemed to know everything. The Juban district had in total just over twenty-six thousand people and my village had less than one thousand, so we knew everyone, and everyone knew us. It was small and poor but a very pretty village, just by the Sorsogon Bay. When there was a wedding or a funeral or a birth, people did not send invitations, they just assumed that news of the new event would get around and people would show up in time for the reception. It would be rude to invite some people and not others, as the community would bring food and drinks to help the hosts with the party.

Unfortunately, most of the events were sad, with the elderly passing away. The youngsters, like myself, would leave to go to school in a larger town or even to university in Sorsogon City or Manila, and get married and have babies there, so the amount of new parties for happy events was declining.

I was considered an exception. I grew up in my village and, like most people, went to school in Sorsogon City. I was living with my uncle and aunt – my cousin Grace's parents – in Sorsogon during my first year at university. They were nice people who treated me kindly and I found it very easy to adapt to a larger town and a new way of life. I would call my parents once a week, as my aunt would allow me to use her phone for free. My aunt is my mother's sister and all her children had left home, either to work in the capital or abroad, as was the case with my cousin Grace. I naturally took over Grace's old room and my aunt was happy to have a girl in the house again to keep her company.

While I went to Sorsogon, my only other sister got married and moved to Manila with her husband. My parents had empty nest syndrome but were overjoyed to see their daughters moving on with their lives and finally enjoyed having some freedom in their own house. My father was much older than my mother but they both looked to be about the same age. Some said it was because I gave my mother a hard time when I was a child and she aged thirty years in ten. Yes, I was a bit of a troublemaker in my younger days, but I suspected there was something very wrong with my mother's health, even though she always refused to see a doctor.

One evening, when I was studying for final exams, my aunt called my name. I thought it was strange that she called me Aubrey. She normally called me *dear, darling, sweetie,* or anything else gentle and lovely. This time, she used my name and I instantly knew something was wrong. I left my books in the tiny room at the back of the house, crossed the small kitchen, and saw my aunt and uncle sitting on the sofa next to the window. My aunt gestured for me to sit on the cushion by her feet and held my hand tightly.

'Sweetie,' she murmured. 'I am afraid I have bad news.'

My eyes immediately filled with tears and I held my breath, expecting a death in the family. A long silence took over the room, awful thoughts went through my head, and it felt like forever until she spoke again.

'Your mother is very ill, my dear,' she said, looking at me.

'She is not dead?' I shouted.

My uncle's face became as white as a bed linen. He shook his head and snapped at me, 'How dare you wish such evil upon your own mother?'

I mumbled some incoherent words, my mind racing, trying to compose a sentence that would explain that I was, in fact, relieved by the news that my mother was not dead, instead of wishing for it and being disappointed that she was only sick.

My aunt held my hand tightly and, looking at her husband, said, 'She is just shocked and relieved, husband. It is hard on her, now that she will have to go home and look after her mother.'

Now it was my turn to pale and shake my head in disbelief.

'Your mother had a stroke and needs full-time care,' my aunt said. 'Your father cannot look after her alone. You know that your mother was always in charge of the house and your father never washed a dish in his life. You mother cannot walk or talk. Her left side is paralysed and disfigured, and she will need help with the smallest things, such as bathing and brushing her teeth. Your exams finish next week. You go ahead, complete them, and lock your place in the university until your mother... gets better and you can return.'

We looked at each other and we both knew that my mother would never recover. Strokes were irreversible.

'You can come back and live with us anytime, darling,' my aunt said. 'For this week, your parents' next-door neighbour agreed to look after your mother, and your father will stay with a friend. I will book the bus ticket for you to return home next Saturday.'

And so, I endured one more week at university, knowing it was going to be the last week of my studies. At the age of twenty, I became my parents' caregiver. When the bus in which I was returning arrived at my village, there was an entourage of around forty people waiting for me. I had not seen these faces in one year and they all looked very happy to see me. I guess I was the news of the day. Maybe I was the news of the century: the youngster who came back to the village for good.

The days passed by and the house chores were boring. I missed school, my friends, and life in the big city. The only relief was to take my mother to the doctor in the nearby district once every other month. We called it the "trip to Barcelona", as this was the name of the area and city we went to. Whenever I had a break at home, I would go to the internet cafe and chat with people, telling them that I was living in Barcelona, Spain, and making up stories which took me away from the harsh reality at home.

About five months after my mother's stroke, the doctor in Barcelona said he suspected something else was wrong with her and asked for more exams. However, we unfortunately could not pay for the ambulance costs or for the expensive MRI scans he requested. Mother became more and more frail, cried in pain at night, and ten months after her stroke, she passed away while sitting in front of the television, her eyes open, her face pale and twisted.

The funeral was immensely sad, and my father could not stop crying. The entire village came to pay their respects, and as I stood in front of a line of people to shake hands with them, I asked myself what would become of my life. There were at least another fifty people lined up to shake my hand and say comforting words to me and my father when a young hand grabbed mine. I quickly raised my head and saw, to my immense surprise, my cousin Grace's face smiling at me.

We hugged for a long, long time; she patted my head, kissed my cheeks, and could not stop smiling at me. In an environment where everything was sad, and people were crying, this was refreshingly soothing. Not because I was not sad about my mother's death, but because, having looked after her for ten months and seeing her suffer night and day, I was grateful that she was finally at rest and at peace in a better place.

Grace took me away from my father's side and we ran to the back of the house where no one would bother us. We caught up on each other's lives over the last couple of years; I heard about her adventures in Dubai and she heard about my university days and my mother's sickness. We did not realize the time had passed by so quickly until my aunt opened the kitchen door and yelled at us to get inside, because they were about to leave.

'But you have to go already? You just got here!' I cried at Grace.

'Sorry,' she replied. 'But wait. I just had an idea. Why don't you come with me to Dubai? I will stay in the Philippines for another two weeks and I can help you look for a job there. Maybe you can come and work for same cleaning agency as me. Come live with me!'

'But I cannot leave my father here. Who will look after him?'

'He can go and live with my parents. Or with another relative.'

Grace was ecstatic, so full of excitement it was almost contagious.

'I am not so sure,' I said. 'He is high-maintenance. It is all very sudden... we have so much to take care of... and I still have to finish university.'

'Why do you want a degree?' she asked. 'Look at me. I went to college, I have a diploma in Social Studies, and the only job I could get was as a Sales Assistant at Robinsons' department store. What you need is to make as much money as quickly as possible and then open your own business. In Dubai, they will pay you three or four times what you will get here after you get a degree. So, think about the money you will save going to university for three more years and add that to two years in Dubai. That should give you a good start. Maybe you will even meet a nice husband there.'

'But how would I get a job?'

'No worries, I will help you.'

And with that last comment, she smiled at me and went inside to talk to her mother. After much discussion, they agreed to spend the night in the village and head back to Sorsogon the next day. My father, aunt, and uncle spent the evening chatting in the living room, discussing what Father wanted to do next and where he should live. I spent the evening with Grace in my room, dreaming of a new life abroad and making plans to apply for a job. Grace mentioned that she had the application forms back in Sorsogon and as soon as she went back to Dubai at the end of her holiday, she would put in a good word for me with her boss, so he would speed up the process for my recruitment.

The next morning, over breakfast, Father announced that if I were to go away to university or abroad for work, he would move in with his brother, who lived in San Jose Del Monte, just north of Manila. He claimed this house was full of memories of Mother and he needed to find a new job anyway. His brother was a carpenter and he felt he could help with the work without being a burden to him.

The word *burden* was heavy and full of meaning, especially to me. Father knew that if he stayed, I would not go anywhere so as not to leave him alone. My sister was pregnant at the time and had her own family to look after. I could not have asked her to look after Father, as she and her husband lived in a miniscule house, which was going to be very crowded with the arrival of the baby in a few months.

My aunt, uncle, and Grace left for Sorsogon the following morning, and the subsequent week passed very quickly, as I was selling the house's furniture and packing Father's belongings. By the end of the week, I had filled out all the forms for work and gotten the needed references. Two weeks later, Grace left for Dubai with my paperwork, Father moved in with his brother, and I went to my aunt's house once again, this time not knowing when I would leave or where I would be going.

The application process took forever. Days became weeks, which in turn became months. The university year was going to start in three weeks and I still had the chance to enrol and join the second year of Business Administration. I had been waiting for news from Grace before deciding anything, as Dubai was my first option. Then one day, my aunt called my name. I knew it was important but not bad news, as she said "Aubrey, dear," and not just my name. I crossed the kitchen like a cannonball and ran to her with a smile on my face.

'What is it, Auntie?'

'The email! The email has arrived!' She handed her laptop to me and I read it as fast as I could.

*Dear Aubrey,*

*Things are looking good. The recruiter will be in town from the 15th to the 20th of the month. Below is his name and contact details. Have your medical documents ready, polish your English, and remember to be presentable and polite. Do not ask too many questions and make sure you mention my name and my boss' name: Wasim. He owes me a favour and said he would speed things up to get you here. Good luck, dear cousin.*

*Lots of love,*

*Grace*

My heart felt like it was going to explode with excitement. The recruiter would arrive in two days' time and there was a lot I needed to get done. The following morning, my aunt and I went to collect the passport I had applied for weeks ago, and I also got a haircut to look more presentable at the interview. I realised that I had not indulged myself with any new clothes, a new haircut, or even put any makeup on my face since my mother got sick. It felt good to be ecstatic about the dream of a life in Dubai.

In the late afternoon, the recruiter called and informed me of the time and place for the interview. Auntie agreed to let me borrow her black suit, so I would look smart. I was considerably smaller than her, and therefore, had to spend the following day altering the trousers and jacket in a way that would fit me, but also allowed me to reverse it back to its original size after the interview. In the end, the trousers fit well but the jacket was still too big, and I decided to just wear a shirt with pretty white buttons for the big event.

The morning of the interview arrived, and I barely slept the night before. The venue was not too far from my aunt's house and although my interview was booked for seven forty-five in the morning, I decided to leave home at five, just to be on the safe side. The journey was uneventful, and I took the time on the bus to revise the notes in English I was carrying with me. I prayed that the interview itself would not be in English, as I feared that I would not be able to pass. The English we learned in school was fine, but far from professional and conversational. I knew I could fake a few words and get by with basic instructions, which is all Grace said I would need on a day-to-day basis. Thus, the bus journey was all about English memorisation and praying.

Two buses and a twenty-minute walk later, I arrived at a building which looked more like a warehouse than an office complex. The white walls had not been painted in a long time and the heavy metal entrance doors were big enough to pass a truck through them. Engraved on the door was the number 1346. I checked this against the paper in my hands and decided to enter, despite it being only seven o'clock. At the entrance, there was a reception desk with a big and mean-looking man speaking on a walkie-talkie. As I approached him, he immediately pointed to the corridor on the right, without stopping the frivolous communication he was having on the radio. I did not move. I made an attempt to say something, to ask for directions, as I assumed he could not possibly know where I wanted to go. He told the man on the other side of the walkie-talkie to hold on, and told me:

'Don't waste my time! There are a dozen girls there already. Last door, down the corridor.'

Without looking at me, he resumed his conversation and I headed towards the long corridor. I saw a door at the end, on the left, and heard noises inside. I knocked, and everything went quiet. As I opened the door, about twelve women stared at me, all looking very serious, sitting in the small room with about twenty chairs. I spotted an empty seat, and as I bent down to place my handbag on the floor, the girl next to me told me to go get a number from the little table at the corner of the room. I walked there and grabbed a ticket with the number fourteen on it. I went back to my seat and the chitchat resumed with caution. The pretty girl next to me was wearing a blue dress and could not be much older than myself but she looked tired and run down. I asked her why she had arrived so early, and she explained that her village was about nine hours away from the interview centre and she had to take an intercity bus the night before and sleep at the bus station in order to be there in the morning. I felt lucky to be able to stay at my aunt's house but at the same time, I worried that the competition for this job was going to be a lot stronger than I had anticipated.

Time passed and within the following hour, over fifty women entered the small room to get a number. Every time the door opened, we first expected the recruiter and, when we saw it wasn't him but yet another woman competing for the same job, we could not stop staring at her, analysing her choice of clothes, makeup, and even her way of walking.

All the seats were taken, as well as all the empty space on the floor. After a while, women would enter just to collect a number on the little table, which now had been moved next to the door.

At exactly eight o'clock, a tall man in a dark suit, wearing heavy, black-framed glasses opened the door and called for number one. Very shortly, he was back and called for number two, and then three and four, and in less than five minutes, he was already calling for number ten. Then came a long break and he did not return for the next twenty minutes. We never knew what happened, as the girls he had already called never returned to that waiting room. The man with black glasses came back and continued to call numbers until he reached fourteen. I quickly stood up and followed him into another little room just across the hall. The man closed the door behind me and I stood there, in front of two other men, waiting for directions.

'Have a seat,' a skinny man in a shiny grey suit commanded in Tagalog. 'Do you have your documents with you?'

'Yes,' I responded fetching the paperwork from inside my bag.

A man in a white cloak grabbed them and handed them over to the man in the grey suit.

'I see you are not married, no children, no job. Is this correct?' he asked.

'Yes, sir'.

'If you are lying, you will be heavily penalised. Many women say they have no children but in fact, they lie just to get the job. If we find out afterwards, you will have to pay us back for all the expenses and will be sent home without a penny. So, tell us the truth now!' He shouted, looking angry and intimidating.

'I swear, sir, it is all true. I have no husband and no children.'

Something flicked in my head and I decided to waste no time in mentioning my cousin's name.

'My cousin Grace can confirm this. She is already in Dubai. She works for a man named Wasim. He knows my information is true.'

Both men looked at each other and, without notice, the one in grey stood up and came very close to me. He walked around the chair I was sitting on, analysing me from head to toe, and asked me in English:

'Where did you study English?'

I froze. I was not expecting this, and the words did not come out of my mouth.

'You speak English, right?' he insisted.

'Yes, sir. I went to a good school,' I replied, stuttering with nervousness.

'Very good,' he replied and touched my shoulder. 'Follow my colleague to the next room,' he said in Tagalog.

Was that it? All my fears about English and I got asked only one question? I was relieved and quietly thanked God for my luck.

The man in the white cloak stood up and I followed him into the next room. He did a brief medical examination, listened to my heart, looked at my eyes, and took some blood. He then gave me a cup and told me to go into the bathroom next door and fill it up. I complied and came back with the cup full of yellow fluid and, without thinking much, I asked him why he needed all those tests if I had already given them an official medical report with my application form.

He looked at me, smiled, and patiently explained that he worked for a man who does not like to lose money. He was testing all the selected women for the diseases the UAE government had listed as conditions for not granting work visas. We would have to be tested again once we arrived in Dubai, but his boss was not going to invest the airline ticket money to find out someone had AIDS or hepatitis when they got there. Also, he did not want any young girl popping out babies in a few months' time, so we were all screened for pregnancies and we would have to do another urine test the day before boarding the plane. He also told me I would have to get a contraceptive implant. 'Just in case,' he said, smiling mysteriously, as if he knew some big secret.

The man in the grey suit interrupted us and asked me to stand close to the wall and let my hair down. He took a few pictures of me, first of my face and then my full body, and handed me some more forms to be filled out and a contract outlining the type of work and the conditions of the job. I was sent to the room across the hall from the interview room, where three other women were filling out forms. As I walked in, I heard the big man calling number seventeen. I guessed they quickly discarded applicants number fifteen and sixteen while I was doing the medical check-up.

It took me almost two hours to read all the documents and sign them. When I finished and handed over the documents to the big man, I saw that the pre-interview waiting room was still full, as more women kept arriving. Competition was fierce, and I felt lucky that Grace had helped me get so far. Dubai was indeed a dream for many people. The next steps in the process were to submit my passport within the following week and wait for travel details within the next month.

Time passed very slowly in the following five weeks. I kept myself busy, studying English and writing letters to family and friends explaining my upcoming travel plans. Auntie gave me some money to buy new clothes and a suitcase. The recruiting agency advised us to bring only one suitcase, as storage in the new accommodation would be limited. They said the rooms were shared between four and eight women, although Grace told me she knew cases of twelve people sharing the same room.

The day the package with the travel details arrived was beautiful, sunny, and clear, without a single cloud in the sky. If I were superstitious and believed in signs, this would be a great indication of the good fortune to come. The package had my airline ticket, visa documentation, passport, details of the accommodation, and a list of things to bring or not bring. Many types of medications were not allowed, as they were considered drugs and nothing with pornographic content could be brought over, be it a book, DVD, or sex toy. I was also told that casino chips and laser pointers would be confiscated at customs. Apparently, the chips were banned because gambling was forbidden in that country and the laser was for military airspace safety reasons, even though this last one sounded more like an urban myth to me. But who was I to judge? I had never travelled on an airplane before and I was determined to follow every rule by the book and not risk blowing my chance.

Two weeks later, I had my suitcase packed and my aunt took me to the main bus station for the long trip to Dubai. The first step was to get to Manila, around five hundred kilometres away from Sorsogon. I changed intercity buses twice and then took another bus from the main station to the airport. Changing from one bus to another was easy but the departure and arrival timetables were unreliable, and mostly incorrect, which meant my trip lasted nineteen hours overall, with several of those hours spent just sitting around and waiting. I was exhausted from the long journey, as I had not slept on the crowded bus and only ate the packed lunch my aunt had made for me.

This was my first time at an airport and seeing those big metal structures flying in the air was scary and fascinating. Hunger and exhaustion were masked by the excitement of knowing I would soon be on a plane. There was a man holding a sign with the agency's name and logo waiting in the main departure hall and he told me to join a group of people who had already gathered at the end of the corridor. There must have been fifteen women there already and more arrived over the next two hours. I was hungry and thirsty but remembered that, in the letter from the agency with directions and instructions, it was mentioned that all ground transport would be reimbursed and that all meals and necessary hotel accommodations would be paid directly by the agency.

'Excuse me, sir,' I said, tapping the shoulder of the man with the sign.

'What?' he growled back.

'When can we go and have something to eat?'

'Go sit with your friends and do not bother me. When the group is complete, we will go.'

Grace was right. The lack of friendliness was already evident, and we had not even left the country yet.

Three more hours passed, and we were now twenty-six women and two men. The man with the sign came towards us, introduced himself as Mr Santos, and announced that we would be moving shortly. We were to gather our belongings and pack everything we had into one suitcase and one piece of carry-on luggage only. I had a little blanket out, which I was using to take a nap while waiting and when I tried to put it in my carry-on luggage, Mr Santos turned to me and said with a mean laugh, 'You are all the same: peasants and ignorant. Shove this rag into your suitcase. They have free pillows and blankets on the plane, in case you do not know!'

Indeed, I did not know it and I started to wonder how big the beds would be for them to offer pillows and blankets to everyone.

'Sir, excuse me,' I mumbled, starving. 'Are we going to eat soon?'

'You will eat on the plane. Get moving. I need to get you all checked in.'

And with that, we stormed down the ample corridor as we tried to follow Mr Santos as fast as we could, pulling our luggage behind us. I was just concentrating on not passing out from hunger there and then.

Mr Santos checked everyone in and gave us our passports with instructions to give them back to him the moment we boarded the plane. We moved as a group and the man terrorized us the entire time with threats of leaving us behind or cancelling our employment contract before taking off.

Once inside the plane, I sat between two girls, Jenny and Erlat. They seemed nice and were travelling by plane for the first time, too. We were all shocked to see that there were no beds but just small seats in the economy class. The little pillow and blanket were there but I realised the spacious seats that became a bed with the touch of a button which I had seen in the movies were exclusive to the rich, first-class passengers.

At thirty years of age, Erlat was older than Jenny and me, as we were both twenty-one years old. She was also much bigger and must have weighed at least sixty kilos more than me. She was almost too big for her seat and she kept bothering me, with her elbow spilling over my side the entire trip.

We chatted and discovered the commonalities that would bond us for a long time while away from home. Our group was all sitting together in the same area of the plane and it looked like a big excursion group. As the plane took off, I found myself holding onto Jenny's arm with my eyes closed, afraid to look out of the window next to her. One hour into the flight, they announced that lunch and an afternoon snack would be served, and I felt so happy I could clap, but I didn't.

The main meal was delicious, except for the Babybel cheese covered in a tasteless, red, hard cover, which I later found out was wax. It was round, and the red wax made it look like a sweet, so I saved it for last as a dessert. I took the plastic wrap off and bit into the soft, red layer, only to find it was hard, with a soft centre of white cheese. Jenny did the same and we ate it all, just like that, because hunger spoke louder than curiosity. It was just at the end of the meal that we saw Erlat pulling a string, removing the red wax by opening it in two halves and eating only the cheese inside. She looked at me and laughed so hard I thought she would snap open her seatbelt. It was the first of many occasions where the true, sneaky side of Erlat came out.

I slept for a few hours after the meal and woke up with an immense pain in my abdomen. I stood up to go to the toilet, but I was not fast enough to reach it before I got sick and threw up in the middle of the corridor. My face was pale, the smell was revolting, and people from both sides of the corridor screamed in disgust. Mr Santos came from behind me, grabbed my arm, and dragged me into the small airplane bathroom.

'Stay here and don't lock this door!' he shouted and walked out.

I could hear him apologizing to the flight attendants outside and ordering the people in the first row to go and clean up the mess. I knew they were part of our group and I could imagine I would not be their best friend after this incident. Mr Santos stormed into the little lavatory, which could barely fit one person and pushed me towards the mirror as he locked the door behind him. With one hand, he grabbed my throat and with the other, he covered my mouth. His face was millimetres away from mine and I felt even sicker than before. Maybe it was the food, or it was the cheese covered in wax, or maybe it could have been just the excitement of being on a plane travelling overseas. However, my sickness was very real, and it was from the pure fear of this man strangling me in the lavatory cubicle. I could feel the anger in his eyes as he brought his mouth very close to my ear and whispered, 'So help me, God, not to beat you up right here, right now.'

He tightened his grip around my neck and I became desperate for air, trying to grab the hand which was covering my mouth.

'If you scream or make a scene, I will seek revenge later, and trust me, you will beg me to snap your neck and end your pain.' He paused, looked me in the eyes, and resumed in a threatening voice, 'I will remove my hand from your mouth now. You will clean yourself up and apologise to the flight attendants. You will walk back to your seat and stay there for the rest of the flight and I do not want to hear a sound come out of your mouth. Understood?'

I nodded and took his hand away. I breathed in hard and felt like throwing up again. Tears rolled down my cheeks, but I did nothing apart from stare at the floor and hope he would leave.

He unlocked the door but kept his back to it, so it would not open. His right hand moved towards my breast, while he raised a finger to his left hand and touched his lips, making a gesture of silence. He caressed my breast for a few seconds, smiled, turned around, and opened the door. He turned his head back, looked at me, and whispered, 'We will continue this another time. Remember... not one sound.'

I started to cry convulsively and stayed in the toilet for a good ten minutes. When I had finished composing and cleaning myself, I walked out and had to face the stares and finger-pointing all the way back to my seat. I slept for the rest of the flight and prayed that Grace would help me out once we landed.

Unfortunately, the flight was not direct and the connection in Doha, Qatar, only served to make Mr Santos tenser and more upset. We were manoeuvred out of the plane and around the airport like cattle in a corral and when we boarded the plane from Doha to Dubai, I begged Jenny to let me sit by the window.

The flight was very short and soon I was able to see our final destination on the horizon. Oh, how beautiful it was to see the sun setting and the silhouette of the buildings turning orange to reflect its colour. My heart filled with hope and a warm feeling of excitement as tears rolled down my eyes. The trip had felt like forever with the buses, waiting in the airport, and the flights. I was finally getting to my new home.

As we exited the plane, Mr Santos escorted the group through immigration and then to collect our luggage and told us he would keep our passports and visas in the office for safety reasons. We were not sure if he meant the safety of the passports, so they did not get lost, or his business' safety, as we could not do anything or go anywhere without our documents.

When we crossed the airport exit door after customs, a gust of hot air hit us all in the face and the short walk to the bus waiting for us in the parking lot was an introduction to the heat and humidity of the summer months in the desert. That was when I started to track time by seasons, and this was summer number one.

# 2

## GHOST TOWN

In a city where 1.4 million people live, where there are cars on the roads twenty-four hours a day, and where most airplane departures happen between 11:00 pm and 7:00 am, one would expect that all the houses and apartments would be occupied. And in a city where people get bored of seeing Lamborghinis, Porsches, and Ferraris, one would also imagine that high-end luxury homes would be very much in-demand and with low availability. I soon learned that this was not the case.

I had been in Dubai for just over a month and the cleaning job was as hard as I expected. I remember when my cousin Grace came home last August and told me about the job, she was very specific about its working hours and entitlements. She explained how the cleaning job varied, depending on the client. If I wanted to quit my job as a Store Manager and join her in Dubai, I would have to be hired by a cleaning company, which would get the job requests and deploy the maids to their workforce on a daily basis. I would never know where I was going to work until I arrived in the head office and got my assigned location from the shift leader. Grace described it as exciting and diverse, and I started to see that she was accurate in her description. But it was also uncertain and exhausting.

Grace said she had a friend who could place me with a cleaning company that provided full-time, live-in jobs. In this case, I would be hired by the cleaning company and would officially be working for them but would be living in a family's home and working in that house full-time. Alternatively, I would be hired by the cleaning company and would work on a day-to-day basis, cleaning by the hour and living in Sharjah.

There were pros and cons with both arrangements but, ultimately, I needed to apply for the one which would maximise my chances of placement in Dubai. The fact that the daily allocations were more diverse did not matter to me but using Grace as a reference made a large and impactful difference in the recruiting process. Having her around in the accommodation would be good, too. All I wanted was a way out of poverty in the Philippines; a better future, even if that meant cleaning dirty toilets nonstop for two years.

Today, after we were picked up from the company's headquarters, the driver took my colleagues and me to different residences in Dubai and I learned the true meaning of Grace's words: *diverse and exciting.*

Eight ladies were dropped off before me, so there was room in the van to lean over the front seat and have a better glance at where I was going to spend the day. Before we approached the building allocated to me, we entered the biggest roundabout I had ever seen. In the middle of it were palm trees, a water fountain with twelve nozzles spraying blue water into the sky, and a metro train passing above it, while on the streets, there was a convoy of buses fighting to cross the busy lanes. Rizalino, the driver, lowered the volume on the radio and told me:

'Look, Aubrey, this is where you will work today: that building just across from the one that looks like a boat and has a ball on top.'

'It looks like an angry building, with its tiny windows hidden away inside it, almost as if the facade of the building wants to hide it,' I replied.

'No, not the white one! The glass building next door.'

'Ah! That one looks much more modern... and elegant.' Despite being excited, I was also worried about the size of the job. 'But it will be a miracle for me to clean all thirteen apartments in one day,' I said. 'I imagine they must be tiny, studio apartments.'

'Big mistake,' added a woman in the back of the van. 'They are quite large. Most of them are duplexes with two, three, and even four bedrooms. But do not worry. This client only hires our services once a month because the apartments are empty. I've cleaned them once before and managed to finish them all. You will be fine,' she said in an encouraging, motherly tone.

I nodded, trying to imagine why someone would want a cleaner to come to an empty apartment. And why would these apartments be empty, anyway?

Rizalino pulled over into the delivery bay and told me to get going. My job sheet instructed me to ask for Mr Omar at the reception desk. The man at the gate asked for my identification, made me sign a registration book, and called the telephone number on my job sheet. I was told I should go to the ground floor and wait at the main reception desk for Mr Omar.

I walked through the big metal door, crossed the garage, and reached the elevator area. I pressed the button, waited, and when the elevator arrived, I was in shock. It was beautiful! All four walls were glass, with a little TV on top showing the floor numbers, as well as news and ads related to the building. I reached the ground floor, and the place looked like a hotel, complete with a reception desk staffed with attendants in one corner, a bellboy carrying someone's luggage, and valet attendants waiting for the next car to enter.

'Are you Aubrey, from the cleaning agency?' A deep voice with a heavy accent said behind me.

'Yes,' I said, turning around.

'Follow me,' the man said without looking into my eyes.

He started to walk back to the elevator with a bunch of keys in his right hand and some more keys stuck in a paper envelope in his left hand. He looked Indian to me or maybe Bangladeshi, with his dark complexion and straight black hair. He was dressed in a well-tailored suit and had an air of importance to him, which made me think he could be the owner of the property. The elevator stopped at the ninth floor and I followed him out until we reached a seating area in the middle of the corridor.

'Your job here is to clean these apartments,' he commanded. 'They are empty, so all you have to do is to wipe the dust off the kitchen counter, vacuum the floor, and clean the sinks and toilets. Pay special attention to the toilets, as they stink because of the stale water. You should boil up a pot of water and drop it in the sink, so it will wash the bad smell away from the pipes. There is a kettle and all the cleaning materials you will need in apartment 905. You should start with that one, and once you finish, you should go immediately to apartment number 917. I will be waiting for you here on this sofa in one hour, to take you to your next set of apartments.' He paused, looking angry. 'Do you understand me?'

'Yes, sir,' I answered as quickly as I could.

'Good. I am giving you thirty minutes to clean each apartment because these are your first two. You will have to move much faster with the others, as you have to be out of here by five o'clock and the other apartments are much larger than these.' He paused again, took a deep breath, and clapped his hands twice. 'So, get going!'

He placed a set of keys in my hand with the tag reading #917 and walked to the door of the first apartment. While opening the door, he gave me a strange look, one which analysed me from head to toe and put a smirk on his face.

I entered the apartment, rushing to the closet that had the cleaning products in it. The door closed behind me and I realized I was alone. This was a large three-bedroom apartment and I doubted I would be able to finish it on time. It was a beautiful place, with shiny marble floors, mahogany wooden cabinets, and a glass-and-steel staircase. In front of me, there was a huge floor-to-ceiling window looking straight out at the Sheikh's palaces. This must have been the back of the apartment building and even though all the houses looked more like mansions in the background, the two palaces stood out, with their huge structures, glowing sand colour, and dashes of gold on the main facade, sparkling in the sun. Time was of the essence, so I quit the touristic appreciation and started to work straight away.

It was not difficult to find the toilets. The smell emanating from them was disgusting, and even after cleaning them and pouring two pots of boiling water into them, the smell still impregnated my nostrils. My watch ticked away. I vacuumed and mopped the floor frantically and, forty minutes after I had entered apartment 905, I collected all the cleaning materials and headed to the next apartment, number 917.

Thankfully, this apartment was smaller, and I felt confident about doing it in twenty minutes. The routine was the same as in the previous apartment, and I planned to turn on the boiler immediately after I entered, so by the time I finished the upper floor, the toilet and sink would be already properly boiled out.

Mr. Omar walked in without knocking and scared the hell out of me. My time was up, and he waited by the front door impatiently for me to gather the tools and move on to the next apartment.

'May I ask you a question, Mr Omar?'

'Go on,' he replied, the tone of his voice urging me to be quiet.

'Why are all these apartments empty?'

'Listen, girl, I am only the driver. I do not own these apartments.' He was clearly upset and made no effort to hide it from me. 'My boss owns them, and I am here only to make sure you do a good job. Stop talking and let's move on to the next place.'

I followed him, biting my lip and thinking: *What a rude response that was.* We arrived at apartment number 1112, and this time, Mr Omar entered the apartment and sat at the windowsill, an elevated metal plate of about thirty centimetres which connected the large full-length glass to the floor. He looked pensive and not in the mood to talk. I started cleaning upstairs and then moved on to the stairs. It was only then that I heard music. It sounded foreign to me, but I could not figure out how the music was being played, as there was no radio or any electronic device at all in the apartment.

'This is magic!' I exclaimed, looking at Mr Omar for an answer.

'No, that is actually the wrong use of the English language. You should say: *This is magical...* as in a magical song. I know, Indian songs may sound the same, but just look at all the Bollywood movies and the dancing actors. No wonder we all love it... the music is really magical.'

'The music is nice, and magical, I suppose,' I replied sheepishly. 'But I really meant the way the music is playing. I don't see any radios or speakers. How do you do it?'

The music seemed to have changed Mr Omar's mood. Now more relaxed and with a little smile, he answered, 'As this is a state-of-the-art apartment, all the rooms come equipped with built-in speakers and there is a multimedia device below the stairs. All you must do is press this button on the wall and it switches the device on. Sort of a hidden radio.'

'Ah! I feel silly,' I said, trying to be friendly, remembering how harsh he had been just one hour ago. 'It is just that I've never heard of anything like that before.'

'No worries, girl. I had not heard of one either until I came here. My name is Omar, by the way.'

'I know, Mr Omar.'

'Sorry if I was a bit dry with you earlier. It is just that there is a lot of work to be done and I do not want to slow you down.'

I nodded, wondering to myself whether I should respond. Maybe I should be wise, keep quiet, and do the work. I might even get a tip.

'So, let's get moving,' Mr Omar said while opening the door and moving on to the next apartment. 'We will do the following: I'll talk, and you'll clean.'

*That sounds like a good idea*, I thought, but I only replied with a smile.

As we entered apartment number 1713, I could smell the putrid odour coming from the toilet by the entrance hall. I just could not resist and after I took a deep breath, I said in one go, 'So, Mr Omar, why are these apartments closed? They look very nice. I am sure there are people who would like to live in them.'

'There are always people who would like to live in them,' he smiled back at me. 'The owner is a very rich Kuwaiti businessman, who bought twenty-three apartments in this building as an investment two years ago. On those days, the property market was booming, and before this building was even announced for sale, many friends of the constructors,' he said, winking at me at the word *friends*, 'had the opportunity to buy a property at a fraction of the price. Some people bought several units without even knowing the specification or size of the apartments. My boss was one of them. He bought twenty-three units in one go on a Tuesday afternoon, putting down a twenty percent deposit for them. The showroom was going to open on that same week, on a Thursday, and he asked me to drive him there one hour after the opening. I knew some of my driver colleagues were asked by their bosses to go and stand in line, so their bosses would be the first ones into the showroom in order to pick the best units available. My cousin, who works for a businessman in Al-Ain, stood in line for more than thirty hours securing a place for his boss.'

'But how is that possible?' I asked, a bit overwhelmed with his story. 'How did he sleep and eat?'

'He had a blanket and slept on the sidewalk. His boss sent a maid twice a day with water and some food. Even being there thirty hours earlier, he did not manage to secure his boss a position amongst the first ten people going into the showroom. But my boss was wiser and understood the property game. At ten in the morning on the official day of the showroom opening, I drove him here, to this very place. There was no building built yet, only a white office with a queue of people going around the block. The drivers had left, and all their patrons were now in line waiting to be served. A lot of confusion was going on ...'

Mr Omar had stopped talking as he realised I had already finished that floor and was moving upstairs.

'You work even faster when listening to a good story,' he said to me, pleased with the progress I'd made. 'Where was I? Yes, I was saying that there was a lot of confusion outside on the street, people pushing each other, yelling at the security guard at the door, and photographers gathered on the opposite side of the road taking pictures of what looked like a riot. My boss asked me to pull over around the corner, into the provisional parking space made for the event, and told me to come with him. He walked up to the crowd and pointed at a man in the queue dressed in a white dishdasha. The man must have been the fiftieth person in the queue, and it did not look like he would get into the showroom office anytime soon. My boss told me to go to the man and repeat the following words: *My boss has a business proposition for you. Today, one of these apartments will be yours. I will stay in your place in line while you discuss this business with my boss.*

'The man looked at me incredulously and started to scan the other side of the road, where I was pointing, until he saw my boss waving his hands at him. The man crossed the road and after five minutes, my boss waved at me to go to the car. He and the man from the queue walked to the car, too, where my boss opened his briefcase, took some papers out, signed them, and handed them over to the man. My boss told me to go back to the queue and repeat the process. Forty-five minutes later, there were six men standing along the car with my boss, all looking pleased, as if someone had given them a gift.

'Let's move on to the next apartment on the twenty-third floor,' Mr Omar said. He was now helping me carry the cleaning apparatus and walked quickly towards the elevator.

'What happened? Did your boss give them the apartments? Did they pay him? How? Bags full of money?' I was so full of questions that I felt I could go on cleaning another hundred apartments and Mr Omar would never be able to finish answering them.

'I will tell you. Just get into the elevator.' He made sweeping gestures with his hands as a signal for me to hurry up. "And remember: never, ever, tell anyone this. I can get fired for telling you these stories.'

'Oh, so they are not real? Just stories?'

He looked offended and biting his bottom lip, he said in a quiet voice, 'Let's pretend they are, even though they are very real, indeed.'

'My lips are sealed. But please, go on,' I begged, full of curiosity. 'What happened?'

'Well, my boss asked me to find a taxi. He collected all the signed documents from the six men, put them back into his briefcase, and told the taxi driver to take three of the men to the bank. The other three came in the car with us. At the bank, the men made their deposits and transfers and received the signed documents back. No bags full of money. It was all very proper and correct. But the fact is that in only two hours, my boss had sold ten units in this building for an immense profit. The extra money he made meant that, in the end, he got thirteen units for the price of three. A pretty amazing deal, if you ask me.'

'So why didn't he sell the other thirteen and make more money from them?' I asked.

'Because he believed the property prices would go up even more after some time. And they did. He still believes he will be able to sell these units in three years' time for eight times the price he paid.'

'But are they really that expensive?'

'Not right now. The market slowed down, you know, after the economic crisis and all. But my boss thinks their price will recover, and that he will still make a large profit.'

'But why doesn't he rent them out?'

Mr Omar laughed. 'You really think like a poor person. My boss does not need the money. For him, this is nothing. Peanuts, as they say. He got ten apartments for free in two hours doing business. He can wait. Renting is a hassle: dealing with tenants or real estate agents, which he cannot bother going through. Besides, an apartment sold as a virgin gets a better price.'

'Virgin apartments?' I asked incredulously.

'Yes, virgin, when no one has lived in them before."

'Oh, I see.'

We moved on to the next unit and the cleaning process started again. This apartment was very bright and overlooked the World Trade Centre building, with its tiny, hidden windows.

'Tell me more, Mr Omar,' I pleaded in a girly, charming voice.

'I am not sure what to tell you. I feel like I already said more than I should have.'

'Tell me about the white building. Why was it made this way?'

'I have no idea why. It must have something to do with the sun and getting shade whist having a view. Really, I do not know. But I heard that in the old days, when there was nothing else in Dubai other than the old town by the creek, the rulers decided to start expanding the city and this white building was the first one to be built on Sheikh Zayed Road. There is a famous picture that shows a road in the middle of the desert and the only thing there is this building. Nothing else, none of these high-rise towers you see today. This white building is quite a landmark in Dubai, although most people nowadays appreciate the Burj more than the old, white World Trade Centre building."

Mr Omar carried on with his stories, some about the history of the city, some about his hometown in India, and lots of gossip about Bollywood movie stars that I had never heard of before.

I kept cleaning as fast as I could, only stopping to take a sip of water when we entered the elevator to move to the next apartment. At two in the afternoon, Mr Omar allowed me to stop for ten minutes to eat the banana and sandwich I had brought with me. Mr Omar disappeared for most of the afternoon and showed up again at five minutes to five o'clock to wrap up the day. The day flew by and by the end of it, I was exhausted.

He paid me and, as I thanked him, one last question came into my mind.

'Mr Omar?'

'Enough stories. You'd better get going. The driver must be waiting,' he replied.

'Just one final question,' I begged him, batting my eyelashes innocently. 'This is a hotel, right?'

He nodded.

'I noticed they have the hotel maids cleaning some units. Wouldn't be easier for your boss just to get some of them to do this work, instead of hiring an outside agency?'

'Girl, do you know why my boss is so rich? He can make millions in two hours reselling apartments. But he is thrifty and still likes to save a few dirhams when he can. And your work is cheaper than that of the hotel cleaners.'

I looked down, not wanting Mr Omar to see my eyes filling up with tears. I turned around, said farewell, and walked towards the van. There was something pressing against my chest so hard I could hardly breathe. Was it the fact that Mr Omar said I was cheap? Or was it because I knew I would never be able to live in a place like this? Or be as rich as his boss? After a full day of cleaning empty luxury apartments, I was not looking forward to going back to my crowded accommodation in Sharjah. Sometimes, we do not pick our lives... destiny pushes us into them.

# 3

# TRAFFIC JAM

Traffic was horrendous. There must have been an accident on the bridge that crossed the Dubai creek because the van was not moving at all and we were stuck on the border between Dubai and Sharjah. It was going to be a long journey and I understood why we had to leave home at five-thirty in the morning every day, despite never really starting any work before eight.

Rizalino seemed to be used to the traffic and did not look bothered. He chatted happily with Maricar, who was sitting in the front seat beside him. He knew Maricar was safe company and no one would think anything bad or inappropriate about the friendly way in which they talked. Rizalino's childhood best friend was Maricar's husband, who was back home in the Philippines, looking after two of their four children. The other two children lived with Maricar's mother in a house two blocks down the street from their father. At the time Maricar applied for her cleaning job, her husband applied for a driving position with the same company. Rizalino put in a good word for him and was certain he would get the job. Maricar only applied for the job to support and encourage her husband, as she did not think she would get the position. She had been a housewife for almost twelve years and had no references from employers to put on her application form. The plan was that her husband would get the job and she would stay at home looking after the kids. If, by any miracle, the company decided to hire her, too, then both her and her husband would travel to Dubai, as her mother had agreed to look after all four children. The financial benefit of having the two of them working abroad would be worth it, and Maricar felt she would be able to bear the pain of the distance from her children by having her husband close by.

Maricar's husband got all his documents translated and certified by the Philippine authority, so he could enrol in a driving school in Dubai as soon as possible in order to get a local driver's license, and after two months of interviews, he walked into the house one day and found two envelopes on the dining table. They were identical envelopes, one addressed to him and the other addressed to Maricar. She was in the kitchen preparing dinner and felt a gush of cold air moving up her spine the moment her husband entered the house. She dropped everything, switched off the stove where a pot of soup was cooking, and ran to the dining room.

'I saw them, but I decided to wait for you to arrive, so we could open them together,' she panted.

'So, let's get it done,' her husband quickly answered. 'From what Rizalino said, it can only be good news. Maybe even double good news. You first, Maricar.'

He handed the envelope with her name on it to her and she opened it with trembling hands. Her eyes quickly filled with tears and her husband could not read whether her expression was happiness or sadness.

'What, what? Tell me,' he ordered her, impatiently.

'I've got it! We are both going to Dubai! I cannot believe it!' Maricar answered. 'But our children... I will miss them so much.' And she started to cry.

She started to walk back to the kitchen, not wanting her husband to see the tears streaming down her face, when she heard a *thump* from the dining room. She turned around quickly and saw her husband sitting on the floor, holding the other envelope, now opened.

'They rejected me. I didn't get the job,' he muttered lifelessly.

'But how? Rizalino told us it was a done deal. They need another driver. There must be a mistake!'

'It is very clear in the letter. They will no longer hire a new driver.'

They looked at each other silently for at least a minute.

'What are we going to do? Maybe if we tell them I will only go if you go, they will hire you, too,' Maricar said, trying to sound convincing.

'It will most likely backfire and they might end up thinking that you will not survive there without me. We cannot miss this opportunity. At least one of us must go. The money you will earn will make a huge difference and we will be able to send the kids to university. They can have a better life than us.'

'But I am not going without you!' she shouted.

'Calm down, Maricar.'

'No! Our deal was either you go or both of us go. I am not going alone!' She paused, took a deep breath, and continued. 'Who is going to look after the children?'

'I will. And your mother can help. She was going to look after them anyway, if we both went to Dubai. Now she will have help. The kids can stay four days with her and three days with me. Or two of them can stay with her and two can stay with me. We will figure it out, my love.'

And that was the last conversation they had about the children. Maricar would start to cry every time the topic came up, so she and her husband decided he would make an arrangement with her mother and only notify her when it was all done. Her children were her life. She had quit her restaurant job when she was five months pregnant with their first child and had not been away from them a day of her life since bringing them into this world.

At my accommodation in Sharjah, Maricar and I shared a bunk bed and she slept on the bottom bunk. Underneath my mattress, at the part where the metal frame of the bunk bed met the foam of the mattress, she glued pictures of the kids, drawings they made for her when she left, little locks of hair wrapped in cellophane, and a silk pouch containing a tooth. Her six-year-old daughter had lost her first baby tooth a week before Maricar boarded the plane and insisted that Mommy should have it to bring her good luck and keep the monsters away at night. Sometimes, late at night, when I woke up with severe cramps in my legs from a hard day's work, I heard tiny sobs, and I knew it was Maricar, thinking of her children.

The fact that everyone knew this story made her relationship with Rizalino one of love and hate. He had filled her husband's head with dreams of working in Dubai, only for them never to come true. But she was also grateful to have a close friend nearby, and she knew her husband only agreed for her to come when Rizalino promised to look after her. And so, he did, including keeping her entertained with silly stories when the boredom of a traffic jam went on and on outside.

Forty minutes had passed, and we must have moved less than fifty meters. Rizalino announced to the back of the van that he was going to give it another twenty minutes and then he would call the head office to get instructions on what to do, as we were going to be late for work. The moment he finished telling us this, his telephone rang.

'Hello,' he answered. 'Mm-hm. Ah. Okay. Okay. But... I know. But it is hot.'

A long pause and we could see Rizalino lowering his head in defeat.

'Yes, boss,' he mumbled and pressed the disconnect button on his mobile phone.

'Listen up, ladies,' he said, turning so we could see his face. 'The head office just called. We will continue to try to get to work this morning. But the boss already heard about the traffic jam on the radio and told me not to waste any fuel. So, I am switching the van off until we start to move again. Open up your windows... the air conditioning is going off.'

He turned around in his seat and switched off the engine. I could swear I heard him whisper something to Maricar, which I thought was, 'greedy, stingy, bastard boss', but Maricar did not answer back, so I did not question it. About thirty seconds later, she started to laugh. We all looked at her and Mariann shouted from the back, 'The heat already took one victim. Crazy woman onboard! Turn the A/C on!'

'Rizalino just gave me an idea,' Maricar started to say, turning around to look at us in the back of the van. 'Do you remember when Boss Wasim told Lu that in Arabic, the word *habibi* meant *my dear, or loved one?*'

We all remembered. Boss Wasim was an old, fat, sweaty, and smelly man who liked young girls. The irony was, as I learned later, that Wasim in Arabic means *handsome*! He was the manager in charge of the cleaning company and had a job allocation system which favoured his protégés. We never understood why the owners of the company would put a Pakistani man in charge of managing a group of Filipinos, given that he didn't understand a single word of what we said. Lu, on the other hand, was twenty-five years old, had a great body, and the most beautiful, long black hair I had ever seen. She turned a blind eye to Wasim's glances and smiled at him in order to be allocated easier jobs.

One day last winter, two weeks after Lu arrived in Dubai, Wasim told her that he wanted her to change her name. It was customary for people from Asia to change their names to a more Westernised version. He felt that Lualhati was too difficult to pronounce and he suggested changing her name to Bibi. She thought it was a childish name, but he insisted on calling her Bibi because in Arabic, it would be short for *habibi*, meaning *my loved one*.

Lualhati truly hated the name Bibi and made clear to Wasim and all of us that she wanted to be called Lu from that day onwards. She later found out that the correct word in Arabic for *my loved one*, being a female person, would be *habibiti*, not *habibi*. But she never told Wasim, just gave him a little laugh every time he called her Bibi. He thought she laughed because the name was cute. In reality, she laughed because she thought he was an idiot trying to impress her.

So yes, we all knew about the Bibi story, but no one, apart from Wasim, had ever called Lu any name other than Lu.

'From now on, I will call Boss Wasim *Bibi*,' Maricar continued, laughing her lungs out. 'As in the letters BB in English, an abbreviation for *Bastard Boss*.'

We all started to laugh so hard that people in the cars around us were staring and probably thought we were all suffering from heat-stroke induced dementia.

Another half hour went by and we moved maybe ten meters. Something really serious must had happened. The radio continued to inform drivers to avoid this road, but what could we have done? We were stuck. Rizalino's phone rang again and we all went silent.

'Hello! Yes, boss... not moving, boss... impossible. I will call back when the traffic moves, and we can estimate our new arrival time.'

We could see on Rizalino's face that Wasim had given him a hard time. He always did. He gave everyone a hard time. The cleaning company did a fantastic job recruiting. They would send the nicest and most charming people to the villages in the Philippines and present this ideal work environment where we could be proactive, speak our minds, and rely on our supervisors for help and assistance with any matter.

Before I came to Dubai, my cousin Grace told me the truth: That my only friends would be the other women from the Philippines living in the camp and that I should not expect much from my boss.

It was past one in the afternoon and it had been four hours since we last moved an inch. We were still sitting in the van with the air conditioning off to save fuel. The office had given up on calling Rizalino for updates on his location. When the cars finally started to move again, and we saw an indication that whatever had happened was now resolved, Rizalino called the office again and was ordered to turn around and drive us back home. We would not work today and had the rest of the day free.

By the time we got back to the accommodation compound, it was already two-thirty in the afternoon and we all felt happy to have a few extra hours to relax and prepare supper. We were giggling and chatting when we reached home and got off the van and, as we waved goodbye to Rizalino, he lowered his window and called for Maricar. They exchanged a few words and he drove away. She just stood there on the sidewalk, looking at us, sombre and mournful.

'What happened?' Grace and I enquired simultaneously.

'I am sorry, girls,' Maricar replied. 'But as we did not work today, it will be considered a day off and we will compensate by working an extra day next week.'

The happy atmosphere died instantaneously. The traffic jam, so blessed moments ago, was now being cursed at by infuriated and tired women standing on a Sharjah sidewalk.

# AUTUMN - 2008

# 4

# BALCONIES

It was so nice to work on autumn and winter days. The weather was cool and sometimes the clouds in the sky reminded me of home. There were, however, two problems: fog and dust. The fog was an issue in the mornings, as it slowed down traffic and caused accidents. Since I had gotten to Dubai, we had not had many issues with fog and accidents, but Rizalino said that once last year, there was an accident on the main road connecting Dubai and Abu Dhabi and over one hundred and sixty cars were involved. Maricar thought it was an exaggeration on his part but he insisted that things could get very ugly when the fog settled, and people continued to drive at high speeds and very close to the car in front of them. I suppose one hundred and sixty was not an impossible number.

The problem with dust was a different case. There had been a sandstorm the day before and the Madam from the apartment I had cleaned that day insisted that I pay special attention to cleaning her balcony. Her home was in the middle of a construction site called Downtown Dubai. It hosted the tallest building in the world and the biggest shopping mall in the world and it had several developments, commercial and residential, around a lake and a fountain which, in order to keep in line with its surroundings, surely was either the largest, longest, tallest, or nicest in the world. Madam's apartment was not directly by the lake but a block or so away, and all around it were building sites. It was called Boulevard 8 and it was a standalone building with balconies going around its entire circumference.

My time there was supposed to be only four hours and, given that it was a two-bedroom apartment, this should not have been a problem. But Madam insisted that the balconies should be immaculately clean by the time I left and when I arrived, they looked like they had not seen water and soap for at least a decade. Madam claimed that they had been washed the week before and that the sandstorm from yesterday was responsible for the mess.

Balconies were a Dubai phenomenon. When people moved to Dubai, they often came from either a dark and rainy city, where sunlight was a rarity and they dreamt of waking up and seeing the cloudless blue sky and having a cocktail while sunbathing on their balconies, or they came from cities where the cost of living was horrendously expensive and all they could afford was a shoebox-sized apartment, where a balcony would be seen as a waste of space compared to having one extra closet. In any case, balconies were a luxury that most could not afford before and were highly valued by the time they moved to Dubai.

Balconies looked perfect on paper. The problem was that they had a very limited annual usage rate and proved to be of no or very restricted use on a daily basis. Over the long summer, no one stayed outside anyway, and even those good souls who claimed that they would cook a nice barbecue on a summer's day gave up the idea after realizing that being next to flames and hot coal while the weather was forty-five degrees outside was not particularly pleasant. Over the winter, one used the balcony during the day, as the evenings could get a bit chilly. My friend who worked at one of the beach restaurants in a five-star hotel told me that guests asked for heaters and pashminas all through the winter. As everybody was busy working and making tax-free money, there was little for balconies use during the week and on the weekend, they tended to go driving in the desert or hit the beach. So, in reality, there were only a few months in the year when people truly appreciated their balconies; that is, if they had a live-in maid who would clean it daily because they could go from spotless to a sand pit in the blink of an eye.

I did not understand why people would prefer an apartment with a balcony, but maybe my view was biased due to the hard work it took to clean them. Today, when I only had twenty minutes left to clean the outside area of Madam's apartment, I decided to be brave and ask her why she wanted a balcony in the first place.

Madam was not a posh woman and seemed like a down-to-earth person, although all she did while I was there was fix her nails. I approached her while I was cleaning her dining room and she seemed keen to chat while I worked. She told me that she had come from a city in England with a funny name ending in Chester, like Worchester or Dorchester but I cannot be exactly sure. It was her dream to be tan and have the sun shining every day. She paused, stood up, and went into the bedroom to get something. When she came back, she was holding, very delicately with the tip of her fingers so her recently applied nail polish would not get smudged, a picture of her house back in her home country. It was a small, redbrick cottage with only two tiny windows in front. It had a little garden, which looked very green and fertile but not particularly well-kept.

'Oh, I see,' I exclaimed.

'It was not bad, but out here, every day when I wake up, I look at the sky and there is the glow of the sun shining on me,' she explained, almost feeling guilty for having asked me to clean the outside.

'All I wanted was to sit outside, breathe the fresh air, and get a tan while reading a book,' she added. 'But having been here for almost a year, I see what a delusional idea that was. I can go to the pool in the building or to the beach and do the same thing. I do not need a balcony. And it gets dirty from one day to the next, so I rarely use it. But I guess most expats do not know that when they move here, so the idea of having a balcony is very appealing.'

I was almost done with the cleaning and I nodded in agreement with her delusional statement. She went inside again, I guess to put the picture away. After two minutes, she came out back with a funny look on her face, insisting on explaining herself.

'You see, I have guests coming over tonight for dinner and two of them smoke. So, having the balcony will be very useful after all.' She gave a long pause, reached inside her pocket, and put a twenty dirham note on my palm. 'Thank you, Aubrey.'

I was done and packed five minutes later and left Madam contemplating her newly acquired, freshly cleaned heaven which, I am sure, would be dusty and unusable by the next morning.

Rizalino picked me up at noon from Boulevard 8 and took me back to the main office to see if any new jobs had been assigned to me for the afternoon. Nothing had come up, so I spent the rest of the day cleaning the office facilities and washing Wasim's car. I was looking forward to going back to the compound and doing my laundry.

At seven-thirty in the evening, Rizalino dropped us off at the compound accommodation and we immediately got on with our chores. The compound was, in reality, an apartment block where the agency rented some apartments. My apartment had two bedrooms with six people in each room. I shared the bedroom with grumpy Mariann, sneaky and chubby Erlat, my best friend Jenny, and the leader of the room, Maricar. We all respected Maricar, maybe because she already had four kids and knew how to get us in line, but mainly because she was nurturing and loving, and we always went to her when we had a problem. There was also an empty bed, and we knew someone else would be occupying that space soon.

Lu, Honorata, and my cousin Grace occupied the bedroom next door, along with three other women. We shared the living room, bathroom, and kitchen, and it all got very crowded once we arrived home. Mariann had designed a rotation plan, wherein between seven - or whatever time we returned from work - until nine in the evening, only a group of four people would be allowed in the kitchen at once. Four was the maximum capacity of the kitchen anyway and so this group of four was responsible for cooking and cleaning on that day. My team agreed to have only three people in the kitchen, as we felt four was too crowded, so until a new person arrived in our bedroom, our team would be smaller but far more efficient. There was no need to set the table, as it would be impossible for all eleven of us to eat together at a table with only six chairs. Therefore, we left the food in the pots, made our plates, and ate wherever we felt like it, with most of us preferring to do it in front of the TV, sharing a space on the couch or the floor. The menu of the day was set in advance, as we needed to buy supplies and split the cost amongst us. Most evenings, we had typical Filipino food. Maricar and Mariann had taught us how to cook some amazing dishes. Lu was great at making Italian pasta and Honorata was the sweets lady, as she had worked in a sweets factory and shop back home. Anyone who wanted to eat something different could do so after nine o'clock at night or feel free to cook their own recipes on their free day. The truth was that no one had the energy to cook or the money to afford a separate meal, so we all ate together and appreciated the cooking arrangement.

The schedule for using the bathroom was more complex, especially in the mornings. The door should never be locked, and we got used to showering while someone else was using the toilet and a third person was brushing their teeth. The showering schedule was very tight, and people would literally push you out when your eight minutes expired. I was lucky that Grace was the person coming in immediately after me and when I wanted to condition my hair, she would let me stand by the curtain while she showered and sneak under the shower to rinse the conditioner off after five minutes. The showering slots were awarded according to the length of time someone had been in Dubai, but people could swap slots if it was in both parties' interest. That was the case with Grace. She exchanged her good spot for a worse one in order for hers to be next to mine, so we could be more flexible in the sixteen minutes we had together.

Sometimes there was confusion, but in general, Mariann kept us all going with military precision. She convinced Wasim to buy two large clocks and installed them in the kitchen and the bathroom, so no one could claim their watch was running five minutes early or late and use that as an excuse for messing up her schedule.

Once supper was finished, we went on to do our own things - washing clothes, cleaning, writing, or calling home. Some girls went out with their boyfriends or spent the evening exchanging text messages on their phones. There was a large Filipino community in the building and, while the fourth and fifth floors were exclusively occupied by women, the remaining floors were occupied by men and, undoubtedly, some chose to hang around downstairs for a quick chat or some romance.

Nonetheless, Mariann's perfect scheduling assumed a day where we would be home in time for the seven o'clock supper. That rarely happened. By the time we got home, ate, and cleaned up, nobody had energy to go downstairs looking for the love of their lives. We knew we had an early start the next day and any extra ten minutes of sleep would be welcomed.

Today, Lu's team was responsible for dinner and, although we were running half an hour late on the official schedule, I knew I had almost one hour until dinner was served. I went to the tiny laundry room and washed a couple of shirts and a few pieces of underwear and went outside to hang them to dry. The washing machine we had was used mainly for large items such as bedsheets and towels and there was no dryer in the apartment, so we all used the hanging wires installed outside on the balcony.

My clothes all had my name written on them in waterproof ink so there would be no questioning who they belonged to. As each person was responsible for their own laundry, this technique was handy, especially when collecting our things from the hanging wire. I started to take my things from the bucket and pin them onto the wire when one of my white shirts slipped from my hands and fell onto the floor. I picked it up, looked at the side of the shirt which had touched the ground, admired the new brown stain, and could not help myself as I let out a scream, almost tripping over the bucket.

'What's going on?' Grace asked, looking puzzled.

'Balconies!' I responded. 'I just hate dusty balconies!'

# 5

## STEALING TRASH

Rizalino was in a bad mood today. Over the last few weeks, he had been in unexpectedly high spirits, which was a blessing since his good mood meant safer driving and a better selection of music in the van. We had grown tired of listening to the same five CDs that Rizalino had brought with him when he came back from his holiday. Maricar and Mariann almost cried every time they heard the song by Levi Celerio, as they were reminded of the loved ones they left back home. Levi was a genius and was even in the *Guinness Book of World Records* for being a leaf-player. However, listening to it was depressing.

It was only a few weeks ago that Rizalino decided to discover the wonder of technology called "the radio". Dubai had many great radio stations, including a particular one in the morning where the two hosts of the morning show talked in a very funny accent and Lu and I made a game out of imitating them. Lu thought they were from Australia and I thought they were from England. Of course, we had yet to meet a Filipino who could speak better English than us to tell us where their accents were from.

The hosts on the radio announced a new quiz, wherein listeners could phone in to tell them the happiest thing that had ever happened to them. We would never call and waste valuable phone credits on frivolous radio games, but we started our own quiz inside the van.

Maricar was first and told us that her happiest moment in life was the first time she looked at her first-born baby's face.

'Ha, ha. I bet you can't say the same about your fourth baby,' said Mariann with a grin. 'I bet that by the fourth delivery, all the magic was gone.'

'You are wrong!' Maricar shouted. 'All my kids are loved the same way. It is just that the first time is always special.'

'It is called *endorphins*. After being in labour for seven hours, any creature popping out of you will be special,' replied Mariann.

Mariann always knew how to get on Maricar's nerves and never missed an opportunity to rub in the fact that she knew more just because she was the eldest amongst us. To me, she always sounded rude and I thought that she must have had a heartache which was never cured, since it had made her so bitter.

Honorata, the sweet and bubbly girl who shared the bedroom with Lu, went next. 'My happiest moment was when I came here,' she said.

'And mine hasn't happened yet. It will be the day I leave this place,' grumpy Mariann added.

Everyone laughed, as it was so typical of her to say such a thing. I could not help thinking that my happiest moment was when my cousin Grace told me about the job. Arriving there was a different matter, but the feeling of excitement, knowing there was hope in my life and that anything was possible, really hit me when Grace came to my home after my mother passed away. So much had happened since then. The excitement was gone. I now knew that it had just been an escape from the enormity of sadness that the months before my mother's death had engraved on me. Surely, this was not something one should call a radio station and share with other listeners.

Unexpectedly, the radio was switched off and Rizalino whispered something to himself that sounded like, "Happiness is always followed by sadness." He speedily put one of his CDs on and stared back at the road so no one would make eye contact or ask him questions.

Silence sat in our mouths immediately, and after what seemed an eternity, we arrived at my drop-off point. Rizalino waved and wished me good luck.

Today was the Peach Palm House day. Madam was rarely home and normally, it was her full-time Sri Lankan maid, Padma, who told me what work I would be doing. Padma was a nice and sweet girl; she must have not been much older than me, perhaps she was even younger, eighteen or nineteen. She definitely looked like she just came out of high school. She always had a smile on her face, but her eyes did not match the happiness expressed by her lips. I asked Belinda, one of the girls who shared the accommodation with us, what she thought, since she also cleaned the house on a different day than me. She said Padma was practicing and preparing to become a Buddhist nun. I was not sure what that meant but I could not see Padma's beautiful and long black hair being shaved off and her gorgeous and sensual curves being hidden under an orange garment in a monastery somewhere.

I rang the doorbell, but it took a while for someone to open the door. I almost fell to the ground when I saw Madam standing there and telling me to enter the house. She asked what my name was. I answered. She asked again. I kept on telling her it was not Audrey, but she shook her head once again. She asked me to spell it and so I did: A-U-B-R-E-Y, but she insisted on replacing the B with the D, maybe thinking of the famous Audrey Hepburn. This misunderstanding must have been a cultural clash and it was a challenge for me. I was yet to find one Westerner who had heard of the name Aubrey, with a B, before. Madam sighed and told me to wait by the entrance while she moved towards the office. Just a few seconds later, she appeared, holding a pad of paper and a pen. She asked me to write down my name, to which I complied immediately. She opened her eyes wide and expelled a long *ahhhhh* sound and asked for my full name.

The work I was asked to do was routine and not once did I see Padma. The house looked relatively clean and there were only a dozen shirts to be ironed. The day went by quickly and at five in the afternoon, I announced the end of the day and told Madam goodbye. She quickly materialised a sheet of paper and asked me to sign it.

*I, _____, have received AED 240,00 for the work performed today at villa 11, Frond K, Palm Jumeirah, Dubai.*

In the blank space she had written my name, correctly with a B, and dated the bottom of the page. I signed on the dotted line, thinking this was very unusual. We normally went in the client's house, never interacted much with them, did the work, and walked out when the van picked us up. All the paperwork was handled by the head office which, for that matter, kept a huge percentage of our salary.

Thinking that the odd situation had ended, I was gobsmacked when I heard Madam command, "Please open your bag for inspection." When I did not react immediately, Madam must have thought she originally said the phrase in Dutch. She repeated the command and this time, I promptly stepped forward and opened my handbag, moving the few objects inside around so she could have a good look at it.

Madam seemed as uncomfortable as I was with the situation and without looking at me, she said in a low, apologetic voice, 'I hope you understand, Aubrey. I am not trying to imply that you have taken anything from this household. But recent events call for more precaution.' She paused, as if she wanted to say something else. Then, she raised her head and muttered as quickly as she could, while opening the door, 'Thank you for coming today.'

I walked to the driveway, where Rizalino was already waiting.

'How did it go, kid?'

'The work was fine, but the departure felt like going through a witch hunt inquisition,' I complained. 'I am not sure what I did wrong. By the end of the shift, Madam searched my handbag and made me sign forms. All very strange.'

Rizalino's face turned red and for a moment, I thought he was choking on a piece of food. He noticed my wary look and turned away, announcing that things were going to be different from now on at the firm.

I did not understand what he meant. But then, he was in a depressing and enigmatic mood that day and I learned from previous mistakes that I should stay out of other people's business.

The next person to be collected was Maricar, followed by Mariann and Honorata. They all seemed cheerful, having had uneventful days. The last to board was Lu, and the moment she entered the van, I knew something had happened.

'Follow me to the back of the van,' she whispered to me while closing the door.

I stood up and went all the way to the last row of seats, next to the left window. Lu sat next to me.

'Something happened, not with me, but I cannot tell you now. Just stay away from Rizalino and I will tell you everything when we get home.'

'What? Tell me,' I insisted.

'Shush! Later.'

We spent the next hour and a half in silence, listening to music, writing, or just sleeping. When we arrived, Lu made a sign for me to wait and let the others go first, so we could be the last ones to exit the van. As all the others were entering the building, Lu pulled me by the arm and we went around the building, into a quiet area. Luckily, it was not our day to cook and we knew it would be a while until dinner was served.

'Sorry I could not tell you earlier, but Rizalino will kill me if he finds out that I know,' Lu said.

'So, tell me! What happened?'

'Do you know Belinda? The quiet woman who sleeps across from me in my room?'

'Yes…'

'Well, she used to clean that peach villa on the Palm, the one you worked on today. She had been cleaning that villa for a few weeks now, every Monday, and the agency would send you on Thursdays. Apparently, she was good friends with the Sri Lankan woman who worked there.'

'I know… Padma. She is nice.'

'Maybe, but she is now in jail.'

'What?'

'I heard that the Dutch Madam found out that Padma and Belinda had a scheme to steal things from the house. Haven't you noticed that Belinda went to work today but was not in the van on the way back?'

'No, I did not notice. But then, she is so quiet and private that I don't think *anyone* would have noticed.'

'She was at the main office all day today, being held for interrogation. I just know all of this because I finished work earlier and was sent to main office to wait for Rizalino, so he could bring us all back home together. I guess they forgot I was in the storage room organising the stock when they started to shout at Belinda.'

'Oh my God! I cannot believe it! What did she do?'

'Apparently, Padma would look for valuable, easy-to-resell items which she thought Madam would not notice if they went missing. Padma didn't have off-days and never left the house, so Madam would not think that she could be involved. So, she used Belinda to take the stolen goods out of the house. When Padma was taken for interrogation, she confessed it all, including that she knew another maid in the Palm who had created a false lining in her jacket and would stuff it with small

Dirham notes, which her employers would not notice were missing. Every night, she would stitch the jacket and even when her Madam accused her of stealing, they did not find the cash while searching through her belongings. This other maid was only caught when her Madam installed a secret camera in her room and saw her sewing the money into the jacket.'

'And is this what Padma was doing?'

'No, she learned from her friend's mistake, so she knew she could not keep the stolen goods or the money she would make from selling them in the house. She asked Belinda to help her out, mainly because Belinda went in and out every Monday and knew some guys who could sell the goods and give her the cash. Padma would choose the items over the week and on Monday, she would take them and put them in the trash bag under the sink. They were normally small things, like a watch or an iPod, mainly things from the kids' rooms, which deferred suspicion as the kids were always losing stuff.'

'I know, those kids have so much stuff! You should see their rooms, with large TVs, video games, computers, and the little girl has four boxes full of jewellery.'

'See, it must have been tempting and easy to take things from them. Towards the end of her day, Belinda would take the trash out but instead of putting it in the main trash bin outside, she would leave it by the side of the house, next to the wall. When her day's work was done, she would receive payment and walk out, with no one suspecting anything. She would leave by the back door, which meant she passed by the trash bag she had left outside. She then collected the items from it, put them in her purse, and met Rizalino in front of the house.'

'Did she admit all of this?'

'Padma had confessed already, even though it took the police three days of demanding interrogation for her to spill the name of her conspirator. It was only this morning that the police came to the agency and Belinda was brought in. The agency seemed more upset than the police and demanded the truth from her even before the cops could take her into the police station. She confirmed it all... and I just sat there, with my ear glued to the door, listening to every word.'

'Where is she now?'

'They took her to the police station, but I don't really know where. They said she needed to give the name of the man who helped her sell the goods afterwards. They thought it was someone from around here, maybe even someone living in the building. It sounded as if the police already came to the building in the afternoon and searched the apartments - in particular, Belinda's belongings. I can only imagine what the others are saying upstairs, after seeing the mess. Maybe they went to other apartments, too.... I don't know.'

'Weren't you afraid they would know you were listening? Why haven't they told us anything?'

'I was shaking on the other side of the storage room door. There must have been six men in the room, shouting at Belinda, making all these accusations, and I heard big noises, as if someone was hitting the wall or kicking a table every now and then. Wasim was also sent to the police station for interrogation, and he left cursing Belinda and Filipinos in general.'

'And how did they find out about Padma in the first place?'

'It was all Belinda's fault. That week, the Dutch Madam had asked the agency for an extra hour of work, as she had more laundry than usual to be ironed. Belinda normally arrived early anyway, following Rizalino's drop-off schedule. The agency forgot to tell her about the extra hour and to collect the respective payment. So, at the end of the day, Madam paid Belinda thirty dirhams more for the extra hour worked. Belinda thought it was a mistake but said nothing. When she handed over the money to Rizalino, she gave him only the usual amount, not including the extra thirty Dirhams. She also signed the book in the van confirming that amount. When Wasim checked the day's total cash, he saw it was missing thirty dirhams. He then checked his request book against Rizalino's receipt book and spotted Belinda's job at the Palm's peach villa. The next morning, Wasim called the Madam to ask if the extra hour was done, to which she confirmed, and he asked for the payment to be given to you, Aubrey, on the following Thursday. Madam was surprised and said she had already paid Belinda for it and felt insulted that she should have to pay for it again. She then became suspicious of Belinda and decided to further investigate the recent disappearance of her children's things, as she could not find them anywhere. When the Madam's husband returned from one of his trips, he pressured Padma to talk, hoping she would say something incriminating about Belinda. He threatened to send her back to Sri Lanka and to go there and personally speak to Padma's strict father and disgrace her in front of her entire family. Rumour has it that she is the daughter of an influential, spiritual Buddhist man and she was sent to Dubai to work as a maid as punishment for her vulgar behaviour back home. Her father blamed her bad behaviour on the way she was brought up by her mother, spoiled and with little respect for her elders. He then decided she needed to experience a harsher way of life with hard work and restricted exposure, hoping that with body fatigue and meditation, she would learn humility and respect. Her father made an agreement with the Madam's husband, so Padma could work in their home. Her husband was travelling a lot to Sri Lanka and India in those days and became a good friend of the Buddhist man. When Padma's affairs were revealed, and her father decided to teach her a lesson, he asked the Dutchman to take his daughter as his servant, but with a few conditions. She was to work for him for two years, always and only inside the house, where she would not have contact with any strange man, apart from the Dutchman and his young son. She should also be allowed two hours in the morning and two hours in the evening for prayers and meditation. Padma's father insisted on paying the Dutchman for his troubles, but the Dutchman declined and agreed to have Padma as his servant only if he could pay her a salary. In the end, Padma and her father flew to Dubai and opened a bank account together, which her salary was paid into every month, but Padma never made use of any of it, as she never left the peach house. Padma's employers were good to her and covered any expenses she could possibly have. She was always well-behaved and diligent in doing the work in the house and following her father's instruction for prayer and meditation. But if she were to leave this life, she would need money and she certainly could not count on her bank account in Dubai, as the moment she touched that money, her father would be notified. Her two year-long 'assignment' was coming to an end and she was going back to Sri Lanka to get a fresh start. Her father managed to hide her past from society, clear her name over the last twenty-three months, and was very much looking forward to having his redeemed daughter back home.'

'And she confessed the crime just like that?'

'She must have been so scared of her father and the life she would have back home, that with the Dutchman's pressure, she broke down and did not think of the punishment she would receive here. Or maybe she did think of it and decided prison here was better than a life there... I just don't know.'

'If she could not access her bank account here, then how did she get the money from Belinda? What did she do with it?'

'The man or men Belinda gave the goods to be sold to would give her the money. Belinda would then, on her free day, go to the money transfer booth and send the money to her family back in the Philippines and to Padma's cousin, who was collecting the money for Padma in secrecy back home, so Padma's father would not know.'

I sat there, looking at the ground wistfully, digesting all the new information Lu gave me. Padma never came across as a spoiled girl and not once had she complained about her job or the family she worked for. In a way, I thought it was strange how she never left the house, but she seemed content with her job arrangement and I never saw anything wrong with it. I suppose this explained why the Madam made me sign a form and searched my handbag. It also explained why Padma was not there. Would I be considered a suspect in this crime, too? I always left by the front door and deposited the trash in the bin as I left, so I guess Madam had no reason to suspect anything of me. I just wished I knew all of this before I went into work that day, so I could have explained myself and made sure no one had doubts about my integrity.

'Why you are being so secretive, then?' I said, looking at Lu, a little confused. 'You could have told everyone in the van. You don't think I am also involved, just because I also work in that house, do you?'

'No, no. Of course not! I have two reasons, really. One is that I do not want Wasim to find out I was listening behind the door,' Lu responded.

'But we would keep this as a secret... no one likes Wasim anyway,' I added before she could continue.

'You are so naïve, Aubrey. People talk, and sooner or later, he would find out and then all my benefits of being his *favourite* would disappear. But the second reason is even more important. Towards the end of the interrogation with Belinda, just before she and Wasim walked out with the police, the officers told Belinda that they knew she had an accomplice who would help her with the money transfer. She admitted it was the driver who had the same day off as her and she thought that he was in love with her, so she took advantage of his feelings and asked him to drive her to the money transfer place before heading to a park or the mall.'

'No way! Rizalino is in love with Belinda?'

'This is what she said. But she swore he knew nothing and thought it was just the normal salary transfer.'

'But we all get paid on the same day and Rizalino takes everyone together after work to make the deposits and transfers immediately!'

'This is why I do not want anyone to know. What if he is involved, too? And if he is not, people will start to talk and then the poor guy will be in a living hell.'

'You are such a good soul, Lu!'

'But I needed to tell someone, and you are my best friend, Aubrey. You have to promise me you will not tell anyone.'

'I cross my heart. Not a word. But what are we going to say to the others when we come back to the apartment? How are we going to explain why we were missing? Grace will shove me against the wall and hold me there until I talk.'

'Just say I got my period, I needed to run to the minimarket to get some sanitary pads, and I wanted you to come with me.'

We started to walk away from the darker corner of the building, turned towards the main entrance, and pretended we just came from the street where the little market was located. There were three men sitting on the sidewalk, smoking cigarettes and chatting out loud. They became silent when we passed, and I knew they were staring at our behinds as we went up the stairs to our apartment.

As we opened the door, Grace came running towards me and wrapped me in a hug.

'What happened?' she asked, almost out of breath.

'Nothing. I just went with Lu to the market to get pads.'

'You could have told us. We just found out someone had been in the house, going through our things.'

I had to think quickly on my feet.

'Did they take anything? Robbers? Were they here when you entered the house?'

'No, no one was here when we came in. They must had come when we were at work. They messed up the entire place, went through all our lockers and cupboards, and even opened the sofa cushions. I don't see anything missing from my things, but you should check that they have not taken any of your stuff.'

'So, you think they were robbers?'

'The guy from the second floor said it was the police. They were looking for something but would not tell him what it was. And then we saw that the three of you were missing. My heart almost stopped beating, Aubrey.'

'I am fine, cousin. Calm down! Lu and I just went to the market. I will go and check my things.'

'Hold on!' said Maricar with a worried look on her face. 'Where is Belinda?'

'I don't know,' answered Lu.

I looked at her and shrugged, shaking my head. A new panic mode developed in the house and they started to talk all at the same time, wondering where Belinda was, and what had happened. Patiently, Maricar clapped her hands and started to speak in a louder voice, so we all could hear her. 'When was the last time you saw her?'

We all spoke at the same time.

'Shush! One at a time, girls!' Maricar shouted, now losing her patience. 'Erlat, when did you last see Belinda?'

'In the morning,' Erlat responded.

'And you, Mariann?'

'In the morning, too, we got in the van together, she sat next to me. She did not talk, but then that is just how Belinda is, an introspective introvert who hates me...'

'No need for name-calling, Mariann,' Maricar interrupted her. '*No one* likes you anyway.' She said it with a sweet voice and a grin, which made us all giggle.

'So, no one has seen her this evening? Was she in the van on the way back?' Maricar continued questioning us.

We all looked at each other in disbelief. How come we never noticed her absence? Rizalino must have known, as he always counted us before taking the highway back home. Today, he was in a strange mood and I now knew why. Could he have known all along about Padma's arrest, even before Belinda?

There were too many questions and Lu and I made sure we escaped the conspiracy theory talks in the living room by claiming we needed to check our cabinets. We were forced to listen to the speculation over dinner but we both went to bed early to avoid any trouble.

The next morning, at the usual time, a new driver came to pick us up. We were all in shock. Lu and I avoided sitting next to each other in order to resist the temptation of talking about Rizalino's role in the robbery. The new driver just told us Rizalino could not make it today, without giving any explanation why, and said he had been hired to drive us for only two days.

Upon arrival at the head office, instead of going straight to the changing room and getting our assignments for the day, we were called to the training room, a medium-sized room at the end of the corridor, with walls painted blue and a small window looking out on the desert. The room was too small to accommodate all of us comfortably, but we managed to squeeze ourselves into it and sat on the carpeted floor. Mr Ali, the owner of the agency, walked in, followed by Wasim, who looked pale, with bags under his eyes. We had never met Mr Ali before. He was a tall man, dressed in a dishdasha so white that it made him glow when he entered the room. He had a strong presence and stood in front of us for a good minute, maybe a minute and a half, in silence, just staring at us, as if trying to read our minds.

'Good morning,' he said politely, in a deep and manly voice. 'We had an incident with one of our employees, and because of that, we will be changing some of the procedures in this agency. Mr Wasim will take you through the new security protocol and I hope you all will comply with it immediately.'

He then stepped aside a made a hand gesture for Wasim to come forward and address us.

'One of your colleagues has committed a crime. Belinda was stealing from clients and is being held by the police. Her family in the Philippines has been contacted and she will be provided with a defence lawyer by the government. Your accommodation was searched yesterday by the police, but nothing has been found.'

I could hear the murmurs in the room, as he continued. 'As a result of this incident, the following will happen:

'Number one: you are forbidden to talk about this matter with anyone. Reporters will want to approach you. You should not say anything about Belinda or the incident to anybody outside this room. All questions or requests from anyone, including reporters, should be directed to me.

'Number two: anyone who has any information about Belinda or the crime she has committed should come to me, directly and immediately, with this information.

'Number three: the police might want to interrogate some of you. They will inform me first and I will take you to the police station. You are to cooperate with them fully. If you need a translator to express yourself properly, one will be made available to you, so do not feel afraid to talk to the police.

'Number four: from now on, some clients will request that you sign a receipt when you get paid. You are to confirm the amount paid and sign. The driver will continue to collect the cash from you as usual.

'Number five: starting today, you are obliged to leave all your personal belongings at home or deposit them in the lockers installed in the changing room. This includes your purse. If you need to carry anything with you to the job, such as water, medicine, or a phone, you are to use these new transparent plastic bags. All your belongings should be visible in this bag. Clients also have the right to ask you to inspect your bag when you exit their houses.

'Any questions?' Mr Ali asked.

We shook our heads, glancing at the small but thick transparent bag with a blue zipper in Wasim's hands. A whispered voice came from behind me.

'Speak up, lady,' Mr Ali commanded.

'Um... uh... I just wanted to ask about Rizalino,' Maricar said, almost choking on her own words. 'What happened to him? He did not drive us this morning.'

'As I explained, some of you will be asked to collaborate with the police,' Wasim explained in a sweet tone, which I had never seen him use before. It must have been Mr Ali's presence, so Wasim wanted to appear to be a nice man. He continued, 'Rizalino went to the police station today to answer questions but he will be back at his job tomorrow or the day after.'

As there were no more questions, we were dismissed and headed for the changing room to start another day's work. The day was long and took forever to pass. I could not wait to get back in the van and talk to Lu. Maybe we would even see Rizalino behind the steering wheel.

But the new driver collected us and took us home that day. And the day after. And the following day, too. We stopped asking the new guy questions, since he clearly knew nothing and was not capable of guessing if or when we would see Rizalino again.

Four days passed and then, at the normal pick-up time, there he was. Rizalino looked pale and tired, with large dark circles present under his eyes but a very large smile on his face. Maricar ran to hug him and tears rolled down her face. She thanked God for sending him back to us and said she had to phone her husband to give him the good news of Rizalino's return. We all had questions for him, but Maricar was very protective of her good friend and asked us to enter the van and be quiet, promising that Rizalino would tell us everything on the way to work.

'I am embarrassed... about everything,' Rizalino said. 'I did not steal anything, but I am embarrassed to have fallen in love with an evil woman who manipulated me. I did not want you to know about my private relationship with Belinda,' he said in a low tone, not looking at any of us, head down, so ashamed for what had happened.

'I was a fool, but I am not guilty. I have nothing to do with the robbery and the police know it all and have let me go.'

'Did they beat you? Treat you badly?' Maricar asked.

'No, of course not! They just interrogated me. I am fine!'

'Was Belinda arrested?' asked Erlat. 'What will happen to her?'

'She was arrested, but I do not know what will happen to her. She was not the main robber, as she was working with Padma,' Rizalino continued and told us the story of how they were taking the goods out of the house and selling them afterwards.

He said that the men selling the goods were also arrested and interrogated and that the people receiving the funds back in the Philippines and Sri Lanka were contacted, too. I imagined Padma's cousin being arrested and Padma's father sitting down in his large and embellished living room, doors and windows closed, his eyes full of tears and his mind full of shame. What a sad outcome for a man who wanted his daughter's life turned around. Would she be deported to Sri Lanka or would she go to jail in Dubai? We all had questions which would not be answered anytime soon.

'So, Rizalino, when did you start dating Belinda?' Mariann asked him with an instigating tone in her voice.

'I was not dating her...'

'But you were so in love... blind love!' Mariann interrupted him, sarcasm in every word she said.

'Yes, I was in love. Maybe something you know nothing about, you cold soul!' Rizalino's face was now red with fury at the way Mariann teased him. But he continued, 'I always liked her. She seemed out of place and like she was not making many friends but, in my mind, she was just a quiet, introverted person like myself. She was always polite, greeting me and giving me sweet smiles when she noticed I was looking at her through the rear-view mirror. It was not until two months ago, when she asked me to take her to the mall on our day off, that I really thought she liked me, too. From then on, every week, I would take her to different places, always stopping at a money transfer shop. She told me she could not send her salary in one lump sum to her father back home because he had a gambling and drinking problem and would spend all the money immediately, not having any left to buy food or pay the bills. So, she would try to send it on a weekly basis, hoping her mother would take part of it before her father spent it all on his addictions. It never crossed my mind to doubt her story, as it matched her quiet and sad personality.

But now I know she was sending the money she stole from clients.' He paused, as if in deep reflection. He looked sad but continued. 'And for the record, nothing happened between us. Belinda might have lied to me about where the money came from, but she never lost her dignity and purity. She never let me touch her or kiss her; we just spent time together and talked.'

Marian coughed loudly, insinuating that he was lying. But he continued, unfussed.

'Once, we briefly held hands, but she quickly moved her hand away, saying her honour was all she had. So, ladies in this van, do not go around spreading gossip and lies about Belinda and things you do not know.'

Rizalino got quiet and pensive for the rest of the trip; a man who, despite being lied to and held in a police station for three days, still defended the honour of the woman he was clearly still in love with.

The Belinda scandal died down over the next few days and we all got used to the new procedures in the company. Almost two weeks had passed by when, one day, Rizalino asked us to be patient, as he had to stop by at the police station on the way back from work. It had been a quiet day and inside the van, there was only Maricar, Lu, and me. We immediately agreed and, after turning onto a few unknown streets, we stopped at a large parking lot.

'Stay in the van,' commanded Rizalino. 'I will be back in five minutes. I just need to end something.'

The moment he went out of our sight, Lu and I jumped out of the van and followed him. Maricar tried to stop us but we ran, and she knew it would be bad to make a scandal in the police station parking lot. Besides, we assumed she would stay, as the keys for the van were still in the ignition and, being a responsible woman, Maricar would not leave the car behind. We followed Rizalino to a large entrance and through the reception area. We waited in the crowded area behind the thirty or so other people seated on the black, rubbery bench seats. About ten minutes later, Belinda was brought in, escorted by two guards, and stayed behind a thick glass wall with a small opening in the middle. Rizalino walked towards her and held up an envelope, which the guard on the right took and opened. It had a few papers inside, probably some documents the firm had asked to be delivered. Rizalino then looked at Belinda and said a couple of phrases. We could not hear them, as we were in the adjacent room and could only see part of the scene. Belinda's eyes filled up with tears as Rizalino turned around and started to walk out of the room. Surprisingly, she pressed her hands against her lips and blew him a kiss. He had his back to her and didn't see that one kiss flying in the air towards him. Lu and I quickly ran back to the van before Rizalino could see us.

All he wanted was to love and be loved. Only once had he touched the skin of her hands. In the end, it took Padma, a tragedy, deceit, lies, and stolen trash for him to get the one thing he dreamt about for months: Belinda's kiss. And even that he'd missed.

# WINTER – 2008

# 6

## WARRIOR'S LIES

I was back from a longer road trip. My work was at the Marina area, a newish part of Dubai with high-rise buildings, almost at the opposite side of the city from the company office. I always found the Marina area to be the hip and young part of town, as I rarely saw anyone over the age of forty there. It seemed like every woman could have been a model and was pushing a baby stroller.

The French Madam in the apartment I went to clean today was no exception: beautiful, tall, and slim with a one-year-old child. Madam lived in a complex of tall brown buildings facing the ocean. I am not an architect or a civil engineer and that might be the reason why I did not understand the construction of these claustrophobic-looking, dark, and unappealing buildings. Being right there in front of the water, one would think they would have built an apartment with full sea views, especially from the main living room or master bedroom. Instead, all the buildings were very tall and extremely close to each other. The views were mainly looking at someone else's apartment and the small windows gave the impression that you were in a prison, rather than a resort-like place. Funnily enough, the best views in Madam's apartment were from the maid's room, looking out onto the beautiful blue ocean.

Normally, this room was full of boxes, an ironing board, and clothes drying on a rack, but today, there was a single bed with a small brown suitcase by its feet. Madam did not have a live-in maid and if she had hired one, she would not have called us to do the cleaning, so I did not understand the meaning of the new furniture.

'Hi!' said a short woman dressed in floral shirt and khaki trousers. 'My name is Kirana.'

'Hi. I am Aubrey.'

'Nice name. What does it mean?'

'I don't know. What does yours mean?'

'*Beautiful sunbeam*,' she smiled and the sun's reflection on her face gave meaning to the phrase. 'Do not worry about me here. I am just staying a couple of weeks and I promise not to interfere with your job. Actually, you will not have to do any ironing today, as it is part of the agreement that I am the one to do it.'

'So, you are not a full-time maid in Madam's house?'

'No. My madam travelled and did not want me staying in her apartment alone, so she lent me to her friend while she is away. I get to stay here for two weeks and I do not have to do any work, as this counts as part of my holidays. But, if I want, I can work and make some extra money, so I do the ironing for other madams in the building.'

'Wow! So, you do not go home on your holidays?'

'I can if I want to. But home is far away in Indonesia and I would rather stay here and make some extra money. Besides, this is like a holiday. The ironing is not hard work, and have you seen the views from this place? It is amazing, better than the Hilton hotel next door.'

I went to the window and took a peek. She was right. I could see the beach and the sea in front of me. Spectacular views!

'Where do you normally live?'

'My Madam's apartment is in a building similar to this one. But the views are terrible over there and all I can see from my room is the apartment in front of it.'

As Kirana talked, I gathered the cleaning utensils and started to walk towards the master suite to begin cleaning. She came along, not helping with anything, not even carrying the bucket full of water. She really was on holiday.

'Why didn't you stay at your apartment, Kirana?'

'My Madam had another maid before me. Madam and her family used to travel a lot and always left the maid in the apartment by herself. Once, they came back home from their trip early and found the maid with her boyfriend sleeping on Madam's bed. It was a gigantic commotion. The maid was sent back home and, since then, every time Madam travels, she does not allow maids to stay in the house alone. So here I am. My Madam is from Spain, the Madam in this apartment is French, and they are good friends. I guess they think of themselves as European... or maybe not. Maybe they just have things in common. Nonetheless, my Madam leaves her apartment keys with this one, so I can go in and collect any clothes I might need and clean her apartment before they return from their holidays.'

'I cannot believe the previous maid was sleeping in your Madam's bed!'

'You must be a very naïve girl. There are far worse things that people do.'

'Like what?' I asked, full of curiosity.

'I heard of a case where, when the family travelled back home over the summer months, the maid stayed behind and transformed the villa she worked at into a brothel. She had several customers every night and, despite the upset looks of the neighbours, no one said anything. The illegal prostitution business went on for the entire summer, until the family returned home. No one suspected anything, and life went on as normal. They only found out when one day, the phone rang and a distressed man on the other side of the line started to cry and beg the Sir to convince his maid to stop whoring. The Sir was puzzled and did not understand, so he asked the man on the other side of the line to come by and explain it all face-to-face. The next day, the caller came by and found the Sir, the Madam, and the maid sitting on the couch in the living room. The man dropped to his knees and proposed there and then to the maid, promising her that if she stopped with the prostitution affair, he would marry her. There was no escape from there, and the man and the maid had to explain themselves to her employers.'

'What happened then?' I asked, so curious I could not contain my amazement.

'She got fired. But she also made plenty of money over that summer, and I don't think she married the guy. He was just a customer in love with her and the word on the street was that she never mixed pleasure with business.'

'I... I... wow!' I had no words to describe how shocked I was to hear such an incredible story. Maybe Kirana made it up. Maybe not.

'Do people really do this?" I asked. 'You're joking, right?'

'I can see you are naïve, Aubrey. Listen, I am telling the truth and I follow Madam's rules very carefully, as I cannot afford to be sent home before my three years are up.'

'How long have you been here?'

'Two years. I am entitled to four weeks' holidays now, but I decided to stay. I only have to hang in here for another year and I will have saved enough for my kids' school.'

'Do you have kids? If I had kids, I would have wanted to go home and see them. Don't you miss them?'

'Oh, yes, so much!' Her eyes filled up with tears and her voice softened. My eyes filled up, too, a combination of seeing her cry, the guilt of my insensitive comment, and the strong smell of bleach I was using to scrub the shower tiles.

'Your Madam would not pay for your ticket to see your kids? How cruel!'

'No, no. And please, do not say this to Madam. It is my secret.'

'I don't understand.' I shook my head and stared at Kirana.

'I am entitled to a holiday every two years and they will pay for my ticket to Indonesia. But I only got this job because I told the agent and the family I work for that I have no children. Some people require that their maids are not married and have no children to reduce the risk of them wanting to go back home before the two-year contract is finished. Also, because it is very hard to keep their spirits up while thinking of their babies back home and some Madams cannot cope with a crying, emotional maid every now and then. So, when I was interviewing for this job, my Madam was very specific about wanting a single and childless maid. I was single... well, divorced, to be more precise, but I lied about having kids. The pay is very good, and I needed the job. I do not talk about my children, but I know they are well and I will see them soon.'

At that moment, the French Madam pushed the door open and stared at Kirana's face. It became clear that the French woman had heard our conversation. They kept on looking at each other without exchanging words, but I knew both of their minds were racing with questions, excuses, and accusations. The silence was broken when the baby in Madam's arms started to cry.

'*Pas de problème, mon amour.* Shush...' the French lady whispered to her baby, rocking him in her arms. 'Kirana,' she continued in her thick accent. 'Come to the living room, please. Aubrey, continue your work here and when you have finished the master suite, start cleaning the baby's room and then the rest of the house. I have to leave for a while, but I will be back before is time for you to go.'

She walked out of the room, rocking the baby, and Kirana followed her, so full of fear that her legs were shaking, and she had to touch the walls to support herself all the way to the living room.

I kept on working and soon moved into the baby's room. It was the darkest room in the house with only one tiny, narrow window in a corner. The white crib with blue lace on the edges was cute and stylish, and the room was so quiet that I wondered if any conversation was taking place at all outside those four walls. About one hour later, I finished the baby's room and started working on the kitchen. As I crossed the hall, I did not see anybody, and there was a weird silence in the house, similar to when someone dies, and people avoid engaging in conversations because they don't know what to say.

I was curious to know what would happen to Kirana. Would she be sent back home immediately? Could they make her pay back the plane tickets or withhold her salary? What was the worst that could happen to her? Questions kept rolling in my head and when I reached under the sink for some trash bags, I found a pile of old newspapers. The very top one caught my eyes and I held my breath when I read the title of the article: *JAILED FOR MAID ATTACK*. I had to hold onto the white cupboard doors and slowly lower myself until I was in a sitting position as I read, mesmerized by the article on the *News in Brief* section in the *7 Days* newspaper:

*Thursday, December 17th*

*LEBANON: a Lebanese woman has been sentenced to 15 days in prison after being convicted of beating her Filipina domestic worker, a rare verdict in such cases in Lebanon, the victim's attorney said.*

*A court in the northern town of Batroun also ordered the defendant to pay 7,200 dollars to her former employee, a 29-year-old woman.*

*"Forensic experts proved the employee was brutally beaten during her period of employment from 2005 to 2006," said the attorney, who works at the charity Caritas Lebanon.*

*According to Human Rights Watch, ninety percent of such workers in Lebanon are subject to mistreatment, ranging from having their passports or salaries withheld to being required to work all week.*

I quickly cut the article out of the newspaper and put it in my pocket. I could not believe the ninety percent figure. Could it be true in the United Arab Emirates also? I was very happy with my working arrangements and, apart from the airplane sexual harassment incident, I had never felt threatened there. But as Kirana said, I was naïve and maybe the fates of live-in maids were different than the fates of the agency maids. Before, I had been thinking that Kirana was going to be sent back home for having lied about her children, but I was now more concerned about her getting beaten up by a skinny French woman. Perhaps the soft-spoken way the French Madam said things was just a facade for ungodly behaviour. I remembered that at school, I studied the history of a French Army commander who wore a funny hat and always had one hand inside his jacket in pictures. The book claimed he was a short man, soft-spoken, but also mad and very evil. He was eventually captured and sent to an island off the coast of Italy. So, here I was, unwillingly associating this tiny, soft-spoken French Madam with Army generals and articles in newspapers.

My blood was boiling, and I started to work as fast as I could, hoping I would get lucky and be able to leave work early. But I could not go until I got paid and nobody was home. Hours passed, and I had finished cleaning the kitchen, dining room, living room, maid's quarters, and even all the windows from the inside. Still, nobody was home. So, I went to the maid's room and stood by the window, admiring the most beautiful view I had ever seen of Dubai. The sun was setting on the ocean and a glow of orange-and-gold sparks reflected on the intense blue water in front of me. My heart filled with peace and for a moment, I dreamt I was on a holiday, with not a shadow of worry in my mind.

*Slam!* A loud noise came from the living room and I felt the hair on the back of my neck rise in anticipation of finding the French Madam. I went to the kitchen and waited there quietly, hoping that I would receive payment and swiftly run out of that place as soon as possible.

'Hi, Aubrey!' she softly said, with her typical heavy accent.

Madam was standing by the door, holding a sound-asleep baby in her arms and smiling gently at me.

'Have you finished?' she asked.

'Yes, Madam.'

'Then please go to the living room. I will put the baby in his cot and I will be right with you.'

She turned her back to me and I decided to collect my transparent plastic bag from Kirana's room before going to meet with Madam, just in case I could leave immediately.

About three minutes later, Madam appeared, asked me if everything was all right, and handed me the payment for the day. She did not ask me to sign any receipt, gently stood up, and walked me to the front door. As she opened it, she smiled once again and thanked me for the work. The minute the door closed behind me, I ran to the elevator and pressed the button several times, hoping the elevator would arrive faster that way. When the doors slid open, I jumped backwards in surprise when I saw Kirana inside.

'Oh, Kirana! It is so good to see you!' I hugged her so hard that she could not move her arms.

'It is good to see you too, Aubrey. But what is it with all the love?' she said with a smirk on her face.

'I was so worried about you. Did she take you to the police? Beat you up? What happened?' I spoke so fast I was running out of air by the end of the sentence.

'I am fine. Come downstairs and I will explain everything.'

I entered the elevator and the moment the doors closed, I stared at her, demanding an explanation. She told me that the French Madam was very nice to her and understood her problem. However, she would have to tell her Spanish friend about what she discovered, but she made a deal with Kirana first. She promised her that if her current Madam got upset and did not want Kirana working with her anymore, that she would have Kirana as her maid and nanny for another year, until Kirana's contract had been completed. Then both of them called the Spanish lady and the French Madam shared the news about Kirana's children and told her she would be happy to have help from someone experienced with kids. Apparently, the Spanish woman did not want to make any decisions now but informed them that she would speak to her husband and let her friend know what she had decided when she returned from her holidays the following week.

Kirana looked relaxed and not worried about the outcome. She said the French Madam took her out of the house, so they could speak without worrying about me, and that she even bought Kirana lunch from one of the restaurants downstairs. Her baby got along well with Kirana and the French Madam was supportive and appreciative of Kirana's love for kids. All in all, it had been a very positive outcome.

'No more lies,' Kirana sighed.

'I am happy for you,' I said. 'But look at this.'

I took the newspaper article out of my pocket and showed it to her. She read it and laughed at the end.

'So, you were afraid I was going to get beaten up?'

'Well... yeah!'

She continued laughing. 'First of all, the French Madam is a really nice and kind woman who would not hurt a fly. Secondly, I used to be a Silat guru back in Indonesia.'

'Silat? What is that?'

'You should know! You are from the Philippines, and you have Silat fighting there.'

'I was never the fighting type of girl... what is it?'

'Silat is a type of martial art originally created in Indonesia, which then spread to Malaysia, Singapore, Thailand, and even the Philippines. It is a fighting style from our ancient, fearless warriors.'

'And you were teaching it?' I asked incredulously.

'I did not teach, but I performed it as a dance during festivals and weddings.'

'Dance? But I thought you said it was a martial art, like karate, right?'

'The movements of Silat are often performed as a dance and can be done either solo or with a partner and are accompanied by music often played by a live band. It is great fun.'

'Wow!' I was impressed. 'Can you show me some moves?'

'Not here, silly! Besides, I have not practiced at all over the last two years. It would take me a long time to warm up and get the foundation postures right. These postures make a fighter remain stable while in motion and I would have to hold each posture for at least ten minutes. So, no, I am not doing any of it here. No way!'

The van came, and I said farewell to Kirana. She was safe and would continue to be, given her amazing skills. But more importantly, she was sane, as the burden of a lie had been lifted from her shoulders. As we drove off, I could not help but wonder what a fight between this Silat warrior and a French Napoleonic fighter would look like. The battle in my head kept me entertained all the way back home.

# SPRING – 2008

# 7

# BEAUTY QUEEN

Once, I woke up in the middle of the night and felt as if a comet had passed by. I didn't know how to explain it, and I guessed it was like having a very bright light filling up the room just seconds before I opened my eyes in the middle of the night. As soon as I opened them, the room was dark, but I was completely awake and rested, as if I had slept for eleven hours in a row. The moment my eyes adjusted to the darkness of the room, I could see several bright little dots floating around me, like tiny drops of liquid mercury suspended in the air. It was a magical moment that only lasted a few seconds, but kept me awake for the rest of the night until the alarm clocks started to go off, one by one, in the room. This phenomenon happened again a few more times over the next few weeks, and I grew curious about it.

It was three in the morning when the comet came to me again. I sat on the edge of my bed, Maricar snoring above me, and the smell of sweat impregnated the room. Normally, I woke up in an uplifted spirit when these comets passed, as the feeling of relaxation was intense, and I knew I could go use the extra hours before the others woke up to get my chores and my writing done. Today, however, it was different. My heart was heavy, and I could not breathe properly. I jumped out of the bunk bed, being careful not to make much noise, and walked to the kitchen to get a glass of water. I downed two full glasses and decided to sit for a while in the living room, in the dark, to catch my breath. As I sat down on the larger sofa, something moved next to me. I leapt off the brown sofa, landed badly on my left foot, and fell onto the floor with a big *thump*. It hurt a lot.

'Shush!' A voice came from the couch.
'Who's there?' I whispered, full of fear and pain.
'What do you mean, Dumbo?' It was Lu's voice.
'What are you doing here?' I asked.
'I couldn't sleep. What about you?'
'Same, same. But what's with being in the dark?'
'I was just thinking, and there is no need to turn on the lights for that.'

I limped my way across the room and switched on the lights in the living room. Lu immediately covered her face and pretended she was rubbing her eyes and yawning, but I could see how red her entire face was. Lu was by far the most beautiful girl I had ever seen, her skin so white and smooth, not a single pimple or wrinkle, and with eyes that were always bright and full of long lashes which needed no mascara in order to give life to her face. The bloated woman in front of me with a red nose and red eyes was not the Lu I regularly saw.

'What on Earth happened to you?'

'Nothing,' she replied in a shy whisper.

'What do you mean, nothing? You obviously have been crying. Are you in pain? Hurt?'

'No, no.'

'So, what is wrong?'

She stood up, switched the lights off, and said: 'I... well...'

She lost her voice and just cried and cried. I stopped pushing for an explanation and we just sat there, lights off, in the darkness of the early morning, hugging and crying. After a long time, Lu could speak again and told me it had to do with a guy she met and that she needed some advice from Rizalino before she could share her story. She asked me to respect her secrecy and promised to tell me all about it that night when we got home from work.

It was almost four-thirty in the morning when Lu decided to go back to bed and try to catch half an hour of sleep before everyone started to wake up. She normally slept in the other bedroom, where most women woke up earlier than five. I suggested she go and sleep in my bed, where she would be able to gain fifteen or twenty minutes of extra sleep. In the meantime, I caught up with my laundry and by six, we were all ready and leaving the apartment for another day's work.

Wasim was his old self that morning, bossing people around, calling Lu his Bibi, and gathering all of us for an important announcement. He puffed out his chest and cleared his throat, as if he was going to make his acceptance speech for the Nobel Prize, and when the silence landed in the room and all eyes were on him, he informed us that Belinda had been deported yesterday and would be tried for her crime back in the Philippines. He was smiling, as if he had won a game where deportation meant his power over us increased tenfold. He went on and on for ten minutes, highlighting all the threats he could think of to frighten us in case something like what Belinda had done ever happened again.

The reality was that we all switched off after one minute and stared at Rizalino, who made eye contact with no one. Belinda's fate was uncertain in a Filipino trial. Recently, the Filipino jails had become famous due to a Michael Jackson's "Thriller" performance in the exercise yard of the Cebu Provincial Detention and Rehabilitation Centre, where inmates in their orange outfits danced the choreography of the song and it became an internet hit. The reality was going to be much harder for Belinda, I was sure.

The lecture from Wasim was over and we went on to our assignments. I saw Lu talking to Rizalino in a corner just before boarding the van and her eyes filled up with tears again as Rizalino placed a hand on her shoulders and tapped her on the back.

I felt helpless towards Lu. Her past was like a Cinderella story turned inside-out. We all knew how beautiful she was, but you should have seen pictures of her when she was nineteen years old. She was the most beautiful girl in the country. Lu was born very poor and her family never had a chance to send her to school. She took care of her eight brothers, three older and five younger than her, and she looked after them all while her father went to work. Her mother died giving birth to her twin brothers, and Lu practically raised them at the age of eight. She, therefore, matured very early and looked much older than her real age.

At twelve, many strangers believed the twins were her sons and treated her like an adult. Her childhood was lost but what destiny had taken away from her in terms of youth, it had given her in the form of beauty. Her older brother quickly realised that she was endowed with an enigmatic look and a gift for capturing men's attention. All his friends wanted to date Lu and her brother designed a plan to protect and exploit her at the same time.

 Her three older brothers, like her, had no formal education. They were street-wise, smart, and had a gift for selling and smooth-talking. Carlo, Cereneo, and Crisanto were inseparable and knew pretty much everyone in a fifty-kilometre radius. After one year of reselling pretty much anything they could get their hands on, they decided to specialise in women's clothes and cars. Carlo, the eldest, was a tall and muscular guy and he would do the buying of the goods. Cereneo was the brain of the group and Crisanto, a little younger than the other two, was the most handsome and was in charge of the selling. At first, the combination of cars and women's clothes seemed an odd one, but Cereneo's plan was brilliant. They would buy an old car which needed a little fixing, something in good condition, sporty, and appealing to middle-aged male customers. Most of their sellers were in distress and the trio became famous for being the go-to guys when one needed to sell their cars fast for cash. Carlo had a gift with cars and he would get the vehicle in pristine condition within a week. Then Cereneo and Crisanto would drive to a pre-selected town, where Crisanto would have already distributed some leaflets announcing the sale of high-end clothes for the fashionable woman at discounted prices. In reality, the clothes were a deal with a local businessman who had several stores in town and did not want any competition there but did not mind making a profit from cities further away. The businessman would provide the brothers with the goods and take a ten percent commission on anything they sold. As the mark-up was closer to seventy percent, the profit for the brothers was very generous. They would put all the merchandise in the repaired car to be sold, drive it to the town where they wanted to sell it, and, on the specific announced day, the women would come running to buy the dresses and blouses Crisanto was so willing to sell. He could convince any lady that a dress matched their eyes or that it made her silhouette sexier and, with his untamed handsomeness, it was all they needed to buy two of everything for sale. While the pile of fabric was surrounded by women, leaning over the car to check the price tags, men would start to pass by and get curious about why so many women were surrounding that one vehicle. Cereneo would be on the sidewalk, pretending to be just another passer-by, and planting seeds of desire in the men's minds. He somehow managed to influence them into thinking that the car was a magnet to attract women and that was exactly what a balding man with low self-esteem needed to restore vitality to his life. Cereneo would pretend to be a potential buyer for the car and sometimes up to five men would be bidding on the automobile, with Carlo taking the bets. Cereneo could easily raise the amount one customer would pay by twenty percent just by playing the I-want-it-more-than-you game. Once the dresses and the car were sold, Carlo and Crisanto would hitchhike back home, while Cereneo would go to the bank, make a deposit, and go home with whatever leftover goods he had by bus. The unsold dresses were returned to the shop owner, who gladly put them up for sale at his store and took his commission money.

It would only take the brothers one big sale every two months to provide for the family, but they were ambitious and tried to make a sale every two weeks. Their clientele was growing, and, in some towns, the arrival of the brothers was a much-anticipated event.

One day, Carlo had an accident while fixing an old pick-up truck and broke his leg in two places. The doctor said he should not move for five weeks but that he would recover completely after that. Cereneo got worried about the business, as they had already distributed the pamphlets of the new sale extravaganza in a large town almost two hundred kilometres away. It was their first time there and they needed the third man to pull the trick of the car auction. As Carlo would have to be homebound, they decided to experiment with leaving Carlo to deal with the kids and taking Lu as the car saleswoman. Lu had no experience with selling anything, but she had a natural talent for being wise and charming. Cereneo, having no other choice, decided to try her out.

At that time, Lu was seventeen years old and looked like a mature woman. Her lean figure, long legs, tiny waist, and plentiful breasts gave her an astonishing model look. She regularly washed her long hair with palm oil and it looked healthy and very shiny. She could barely read and write, as she had not gone to school to learn grammar or maths. Over the years, as she spent most of her time washing, cooking, and cleaning, her only entertainment was listening to the radio, which she purposely tuned to the only English channel available. Her intelligence, allied by nine years of English radio, gave her a fluency in the new language in a way that was better than the lessons taught by many of the English teachers in the schools.

On the day of the sale, Lu, Cereneo, and Crisanto got into the car at three in the morning and initiated the drive to the distant city. The boys coached Lu on what to do and what to say and she grew more and more nervous as time passed. She was afraid of disappointing her brothers and, when they pulled over next to the main square in the town, she got out of the car and started to adjust her top. Crisanto immediately handed her one of the dresses he was taking out of a box and told her to put it on. She would model the dress for him, as this was the most expensive dress they had brought and usually did not sell more than three units of it.

The sun came up and slowly, the square where they had parked the car started to fill up with people. At exactly ten o'clock, Crisanto and Lu, now wearing a beautiful orange dress with little white flowers on it, removed the sheets from the top of the racks full of clothes and declared they were open for business.

People came running and the first two hours were frantic. By one o'clock, most of the clothes were sold and, to Crisanto's surprise, there were no more orange dresses available. They were all sold by Lu, who convinced shoppers that they would look just as good in the dress as she did. Even the larger sizes, which Crisanto always returned to the businessman back home, were sold out. Clients could not stop praising Lu's good looks and she was a strong magnet for the men, too. Cereneo played his usual game of interests in the automobile parked next to Lu, and approached her, pretending to want to buy it. After one hour, she had a circle of around twenty men bidding for the car. Behind these twenty men, there was a crowd of about sixty or seventy men watching the auction. Not long after, the car was sold with two hundred and fifty percent profit and Cereneo could not stop jumping up and down with excitement.

Many onlookers approached Crisanto to ask him where he had found such a beautiful model to display his clothes. When he said that she was his sister, they did not look very surprised, as Crisanto himself was a very, very handsome man, but many suggested to him that he should enlist her in a pageant competition, as the prizes for the winner could be very attractive.

That day, they all decided to take the bus back home together and many smiles and much laughter could be seen and heard in the hours that passed. Cereneo wanted Lu to become a partner in the business and come with them every time. The twins were now nine years old and could look after themselves. Carlos would continue to buy and fix the cars and could stay at home on the day of the sale. Crisanto, on the other hand, wanted Lu to dedicate time to look after herself, her skin and hair, and exercise, so she could enter pageant competitions and make the most of her looks while she was still young and beautiful.

At home, the brothers shared the news with Carlo, who seemed to be pleased with the idea of not having to sell anything and being able to dedicate his time to his passion for fixing cars. Their father had no opinion, or at least he did not express it. He knew his income was not enough to support his nine children and, as the boys grew up and became independent, he preferred to keep his opinion on their work and money matters to himself. The children respected him and asked for his blessings, which he gladly gave to them.

The following month, Lu had already entered, and won, two pageant competitions in her local area. Her beauty, her knowledge of English, and her sad yet inspiring life story was a powerful combination, which won the hearts and minds of judges across the country. Some people started to call her Miss Philippines and claim that she would represent the country in the Miss Universe competition. If there was no competition going on, Lu would join her brothers on the sale day and, posing as the future new Miss Philippines, she attracted a crowd that was even bigger than before.

Marriage proposals came along with Lu's fame. Until then, a big part of the money she had won went to cover her expenses, such as pageant contest fees, clothing, and makeup. Whatever was left was hers to keep in a safe place. Her brothers never suggested that she should contribute to the household, as they saw it as their duty, and recognised the immense sacrifice Lu had already made by raising all of them. By the end of the year, her savings were significant and the number of suitors who wanted her hand in marriage grew proportionally. Her father was very strict when it came to relationships and dating, and denied all requests, saying that Lu would not marry before the age of twenty-one. That was reassuring to her, as she did not fancy any of the suitors and started to dream of a life of glamour and fame as a top model.

On her eighteenth birthday, Lu had a surprise party organized by one of her younger brothers. It was held in the garage where Carlo used to fix the cars. It had been cleaned up and decorated for the occasion. The garage was spacious and now bared no resemblance to the dark and dusty place she remembered. Silver ribbons hung from the ceiling and a cake stood at the far back on a foldable table covered with a white-and-silver tablecloth. Many of her friends came, as did many of her brothers' friends. The place was packed with young people dancing and having a good time. Lu could not be happier and savoured each instant of that amazing party.

At around one in the morning, after the candles were blown out and the cake was cut, she decided to go outside and get some fresh air. She took her shoes off and sat on the grass, contemplating the dark sky. Suddenly, a deep, masculine, and sexy voice came from behind the tree just in front of her.

'Hi,' the voice said. 'Can I join you?'

'Who are you?' Lu replied.

'I am Angelo, a friend of Carlo's.'

'Hm... how come I've never seen you before?'

'I work out of town... happy birthday, by the way!'

'Oh... thanks,' Lu answered, feeling a bit shy.

In a split second, their eyes met, and it felt like a tornado had passed, leaving both of them speechless and completely in love. It was truly love at first sight. Lu knew nothing about Angelo but that did not seem to matter to her. He, on the other hand, knew a lot about Lu, as her brother Carlo had made sure he bragged about her in every conversation he'd had with his friends. Carlo was not mean, he was just proud to be the older brother of the most beautiful girl in the country. Carlo also secretively dreamt that Lu would make enough money to one day buy him a Corvette. By the time they met outside the garage, Angelo knew about the pageant shows, the money she had saved, the marriage proposals her father had rejected, and everything else there was to know. He knew her favourite colour, flower, and movie. He even knew that the best compliment to give her was to praise her long, full, and naturally-curved eyelashes. And that is what he did, sitting there on the grass next to her, as they talked until the night was over.

Time passed, and although Lu's romance with Angelo was not a secret, it was not official either. For all purposes, especially to her father, they were just friends. However, all the brothers knew they had been seeing each other every Saturday and Sunday, when Angelo would return to his parents' home for the weekend. Carlo was excited about the relationship and made sure he covered for Lu when she went out alone with Angelo.

She was in love and time flew by when she was with him. She focused on the work with her brothers instead of the pageants, as Angelo grew jealous of her trips. Slowly, she gave in to his requests and gave up on her dream of, one day, becoming Miss Philippines. She was happy and deeply in love.

Another year went by, and Lu celebrated her nineteenth birthday with Angelo by her side. By the end of that year, she had saved enough money to move out of the house if her father permitted. Her youngest brothers were now eleven years old and she felt that maybe she could convince her father to allow her to marry Angelo if they were to live next door and she could continue to take care of her family. Angelo would need to move back to his hometown, find a new job, and maybe start from scratch, but she knew that at the age of twenty-five, with a secure government job, he was prime marriage material.

She consulted her father and he was strongly opposed to the marriage. He stood by his earlier decision of marriage only after she turned twenty-one and that was still a year and a half away. In fact, he would prefer if she did not marry until the youngsters were sixteen and independent, which would mean she would be twenty-four. She did not want to wait all those years, but she also could not go against her father's will. Therefore, she set herself the target of turning twenty-one and getting a wedding on the same day. It was not the ideal scenario her father had hoped for, but she was certain that the twins would survive without her. She waited, time passed slowly, and it was only the weekend visits from Angelo that kept her going.

That summer, Angelo invited her to go to one of the islands in the south of the country with him. That would be against all of Lu's father's rules, as it clearly implied that they would be spending the evening together, unaccompanied. The country had over seven thousand islands and Angelo said that his friend had a boat which he could borrow for a couple of days. He explained that she would be staying at his friend's fishing cabana, while he would sleep at the beach. All he wanted was some quality time with her to talk about their future together. Lu reluctantly made arrangements for the long weekend trip, including lying to her brothers and father about the trip. She claimed she was going to stay with a friend for a couple of days to prepare for a talent routine required in the next pageant show. The family got excited by her decision to enrol in a beauty contest again and unquestionably supported her, so she could spend three days away from home.

And so, Lu went with Angelo. It was the most magical time of her life. She felt feminine, mischievous, and seductive. The secret trip was the perfect opportunity for her to discuss her marriage plans with the love of her life. As they got to the island, they indeed talked about marriage and he undeniably declared his love for her and agreed to her plans. They also performed a commitment ceremony on the beach the first night, just the two of them, under the moonlight and with the sound of waves crashing on the shore. He bent over, collected a thick leaf from the ground and, with the dexterity of a craftsman, cut it into a little circle resembling a ring. He then took Lu's hand in his and promised to love and adore her for the rest of his life. He called her his wife and they passionately kissed. As the kiss evolved, she felt the lava inside her boiling and heat taking over her body. She could no longer resist her impulses and, as he unbuttoned her shirt and her bra, she gently fell to the ground in anticipation for what was going to be her first time making love.

The next morning, Lu woke up on a bamboo bed with a thin mattress and white bed linen, embraced by the man she secretly called her husband. She was so happy that she closed her eyes and opened them again just to be sure she was not dreaming. They cuddled in bed the whole morning and went swimming in the blue topaz ocean at sunset. Two days had passed, and they grew anxious about going home and leaving paradise behind. He promised her that it would not be long until they could be officially married, and that she should be patient and wait for just one more year to pass. He would save money and they would have their own cabin by the sea to visit on their honeymoon.

The return trip was heavy with anticipation and when she got back home, she went straight to her room and cried silently. Her brothers found it strange that she just locked herself up, particularly as she was so excited when she left on the Friday before. When she got out of the room, she babbled something about the contest being cancelled and that her efforts were wasted. The boys believed the lie and Lu's mood went back to normal for the rest of the week. On the following Friday, at the time when Angelo normally arrived at her house, she waited, prettier than ever, her hair in a tall ponytail and the leaf ring encircling her finger.

She waited and waited. It became dark outside, dinnertime had come and gone, and there was still no news from Angelo. She started to worry about him; maybe he'd had an accident on the way home. At midnight, she lost her calm and asked Carlo to call Angelo's parents' home to see if he had arrived. Although no one answered the phone, Carlo reassured Lu that bad news travelled fast and maybe Angelo had just got held up at work and missed the last bus into town. Carlo promised to look for him the following day and insisted that Lu go to bed without any tears in her eyes.

    The following morning, Lu waited patiently for either a phone call from Angelo or for Carlo to wake up, so he could go after her secret husband. She tried to call Angelo's parents again, but no one answered. Losing her temper, at eleven in the morning, she stormed into Carlo's room and woke him up, demanding that he go to check on Angelo. After much yelling and complaining, Carlo got up, took a shower, got dressed in jeans and a striped shirt, and left through the front door to look for Angelo. Carlo promised to call Lu as soon as he heard any news, and Lu sat by the telephone for the next few hours, waiting anxiously.

    The night had come, and the phone had not rung. Lu became desperate. She fetched Cereneo and Crisanto and forced them to accompany her on her search for Carlo. They asked at the local store and the bar, went to Angelo's neighbours, to the church, to the hospital, and no one knew of Carlo's whereabouts. They had one more place to go before resorting to calling the police to find their brother, so they went to the bus station. The young man at the ticket kiosk mentioned he remembered seeing Carlo that afternoon and told them he had bought a ticket to Manila. Neither Lu nor her brothers knew what was going on, or why Carlo had to go to Manila. Upon much discussion, they decided to go home and wait for a phone call from Carlo, hopefully explaining the situation.

    The phone did not ring that night and Lu did not sleep either. At eight in the morning, the entire family was up and gathered around the dining table having breakfast. When the phone rang, there was much confusion about deciding who should answer it. In the end, Cereneo picked up the receiver and, with relief in his voice, said, 'Carlo! Thank God you called.'

And that was all they heard Cereneo saying. After that, he mumbled a lot of *hm*'s and *ah*'s and nodded vigorously before putting the phone back on its hook. He looked up at the crowd waiting for an announcement and said, 'Carlo is fine. He had to attend to a business matter in Manila and will be back tonight. He said he saw Angelo and he is okay, too. Carlo will share more details when he arrives.'

Cereneo looked immediately down at the floor, avoiding eye contact with Lu at all costs, and walked towards the front door, ready to leave. Lu jumped out of her seat and grabbed her flip-flops in the corridor as she followed Cereneo. She was full of curiosity and could not understand why Cereneo did not ask any questions on the phone, but instead only listened to what seemed to be a very long speech from Carlo.

Cereneo walked out of the house and before he noticed that Lu was behind him, she grabbed his arm and demanded, 'What else did he say?'

'Nothing much.'

'I find it hard to believe that Carlo spoke for almost five minutes and said nothing!'

'Calm down, Lu. As I said, he had to go to Manila to sort out some problems.'

'What about Angelo? Why was he in Manila, too?'

'Listen, Carlo didn't say. He only told me to tell you that he saw Angelo and he was okay, but he is not coming home this weekend.'

'Why not?'

'Lu, stop worrying. It is Sunday and father will be upset if we do not have lunch together. Let's go home, prepare some nice fish, and we can go together to wait for Carlo at the bus station in the afternoon. Okay?'

He gently put an arm around her shoulders and started to move back towards the house.

At four o'clock, Lu was ready by the front door, just waiting for Cereneo so they could go meet Carlo at the bus station. It was a thirty-minute walk from their house and they did not say a word to each other all the way there. When they arrived, the bus from Manila was just pulling in and one by one, the passengers disembarked, some holding small bags, others carrying children, but only one man had nothing in his hands. His shirt had blood stains on it and as he approached Lu and she looked up, she saw Carlo's face, covered in little cuts and with a big bruise on his left cheek and eye.

'Oh my God!' Lu yelled. 'What happened?'

'Come, brother, let me help you.' Cereneo grabbed Carlo from one side, and Lu could see he was walking with a limp.

They walked for five minutes and sat down on a bench outside a restaurant. Lu sat on one side of Carlo, Cereneo on the other, and they patiently waited for answers. Cereneo did not look surprised when he saw that Carlo was injured; it was almost as if he knew what had happened. But he certainly had questions, and he tensed as he looked at Carlo.

'I went to look for Angelo yesterday, as Lu asked me,' Carlo started to say. 'I went to his parents' home, but no one was there. Then, one of their neighbours saw me knocking on the door and came out. He told me that they all went to Manila for Angelo's...'

Carlo had lost his voice. His face turned red and his fists tightened, blood pumping in his forearms so hard that they could see the veins pulsating under the skin. He took several deep breaths and looked at Lu.

'Do not get upset, Lu. I am about to tell you something upsetting, but you have to hold it together, okay?'

He did not wait for an answer from her.

'Angelo got married this weekend to the daughter of a senator.'

He paused and for the longest time, no one said anything, all of them in shock from the unexpected news. Then Carlo continued, 'When I got there, the ceremony had finished, and they were having a reception party in the country club. Took me quite a while to get there and when I did, the security would not let me in. After almost an hour of arguing outside, they agreed to call for the groom and that was when I lost my temper. I saw Angelo walking towards me in a tuxedo and a silver tie, and I knew there was no mistake: that was the same man I once, mistakenly, called my friend."

'What happened then?' asked Cereneo.

'When he got close enough, I punched him in the face. He passed out, unconscious on the ground while I yelled questions at him. It did not take long for the security guards to restrain me, take me to the side road out of the guests' view, and beat the life out of me. A good soul was driving by, saw me lying down on the road, and took me to the hospital. I have three broken ribs and many bruises and stitches but nothing too serious, no long-term damage."

'Those bastards!' yelled Cereneo. 'We will get revenge.'

'Do not worry, brother. That guy is worth less than a cockroach and will rot in hell for lying to all of us.'

Only then Carlo looked at Lu and saw that tears were streaming down her face, but no sound came from her mouth. It was almost as if she was in shock and all she could do was blink the tears away, making room for new ones. Carlo hugged his baby sister, making his ribs bend and sending acute pain throughout his entire body but he did not let her go.

'Maybe it is better this way, Lu. Finding out about this piece of shit before you married him. I am so sorry, Lu.'

And then Carlo, that big man with arms the size of Lu's waist, started to cry. Lu opened her mouth, gasped for air, and cried out loud with him, in a big hug, for a long time, until neither of them had any more tears or energy to release.

Angelo was only interested in power and money and did not miss his lifetime opportunity to marry into a rich and powerful family. He never bothered to explain himself to Carlo or apologise to him for the injuries. In fact, they became enemies, and each prayed he would never see the other again, as it could end with one of them dead and the other in jail. Angelo, however, sent a letter to Lu, wherein he did not give her any explanation for his acts, but said that what they had was *true*. Lu never mentioned the weekend on the island, their secret marriage, or their intimate relations to anyone, as she feared her brothers would either seek revenge and possibly kill Angelo or they would turn against her and shame her even further. Nothing good could come out of it if she revealed her secret, so she kept it to herself, and as a heartbroken, deceived, and dishonoured young woman, she locked herself up deep in her mind and never mentioned Angelo again. She did not cry anymore, but she also never smiled again. She never attended a beauty contest again and when she turned twenty-one, despite her entire family's pleas, she refused to enrol in the Miss Philippines competition. She focused on her duties as a daughter and sister, looking after her brothers, and continuing to go on the sale trips with Crisanto and Cereneo, where all the money she earned was deposited into an account.

Years passed, and Lu never spent one cent of her money on herself. She saved it all and her brothers grew curious as to what she intended to do with the money. Once, one of the twins joked that she was saving for a dowry and Lu went berserk with anger and slapped the boy in the face with all her power. She had never hit any of them before, not even when they badly misbehaved or drove her insane in the house, but this time the boy's comment had touched a wound which obviously had not healed. Lu went to her room after the incident, but never apologised to her brother. That was the proof which the boys had been waiting for, that Lu would never marry due to bitterness and deep heartache.

It was to no one's surprise when one morning, almost a month before she turned twenty-four, Lu asked her father for a moment of his attention. They went to the living area and her father, noticing it was something serious, ordered the boys to go outside for a while so they could have a private conversation. It took Lu a while to find the right words to initiate the dialogue she had planned in her mind for some time.

'Father...'

'Yes, my dear.' His voice was full of worry and tenderness at the same time.

'Remember some years ago when I asked you if I could... um... get married?' She looked down, avoiding any eye contact.

'Yes.'

'Well, you told me that, ideally, you would not want me to marry until the twins turned sixteen, right?'

'Mm-hm.' He nodded.

'Uh... well...'

Lu could not find the words. She started to blush but did not look up at her father.

'Are you saying you want to get married?' He paused, looking puzzled. 'To whom?'

'No, no, no! That's not it. I will never get married again!'

The silence was profound. Lu was not sure if her father's lack of a reaction was because she screamed the word *no* in desperation, or if it was because he had picked up on her slip when she had used the word *again*. He took a deep breath and, probably out of wisdom, only said, 'What do you want, Lu?'

'I will turn twenty-four soon, and I want to leave and start a life for myself.'

'Where are you going?'

'I have saved some money working with Cereneo and I speak good English. I want to go work in Dubai.'

Her father was in shock. Never in a million years would he have guessed that Lu wanted an adventurous life. He was prepared for her to say she wanted to get married, go to school, or maybe even move to the capital, but never to get on a plane and leave them all behind. Only then she looked up and he saw that little sparkle in her eyes, something he had not seen since the Angelo incident. He shook his head and told her that if this was what she really wanted, he would do anything to make her happy. A smile came to her lips and her heart filled with hope.

The following month, Lu paid an intermediate three thousand dollars for an airline ticket and job placement in Dubai. She packed her things, and two days after she turned twenty-four, she boarded a plane to come clean homes in Dubai. By then, her beauty had diminished. Almost four years without paying much attention to her heath or beauty and being depressed most of the time took away some of the glow that Lu had in her younger days. When she arrived in Dubai, she vowed to start a new life and be happy. And indeed, she was. There was never a bad situation, difficult task, or sad story that she could not find a positive side to. She seemed to be an optimistic girl at heart. She never mentioned her difficult past to anyone apart from me, because she considered me to be her best friend, and Maricar, who had been sworn to secrecy. Every time someone paid her a compliment on her looks, Lu would remove the two pictures she always carried in her wallet: one of her in a silver, full-length, figure-hugging sequined dress, and the other; a portrait showing her long hair and her straight, super white teeth. She was nineteen when those pictures were taken and when people looked at them, they could see how much she had changed and aged in such a short time, but no one ever asked her any questions about it. Those same people never praised her for her looks again, and that was exactly what she wanted: to be valued for other things, rather than her beauty.

The morning passed by very quickly, and I spent it working in a villa in a new development called Motorcity, where a racing course had been built. The area was brand new and some houses were not finished yet. The villa I was working in was at the end of the road, surrounded by what would, one day, be a beautiful garden. For now, it was just sand, with a trampoline standing all alone in the middle of it. I had worked in this villa many times before and the nice Madam always gave me an extra tip at the end of the day.

Today, as I finished the work half an hour earlier, she asked me to wash the 4x4 car in the garage.

I noticed the flaps behind the back wheels were broken and asked her what had happened. She told me they had gone into the desert over the weekend and their car had gotten stuck in the sand. The more her husband pressed the gas pedal, the more the wheels turned in vain and dug a deeper hole in the ground. The flaps behind the wheels sank into the sand like two knives through soft butter. They had to use a friend's car to pull theirs out of the sand. The car came out, but the flaps got torn in the manoeuvre. The generous Madam did not seem to mind the damage and said this was nothing compared to what could have happened. She had seen cars flip over, tires come off their wheels, and once, an entire side panel of a car being detached. She laughed as she told me this and all I could think was that playing in the desert must be a very expensive hobby.

Rizalino picked me up at seven o'clock and the van was already full. I was the last one in and he was going to take a shortcut, as an accident had happened on the normal road we took to go home and Motorcity was conveniently located next to an alternative highway. We moved for about ten minutes before traffic came to a standstill. There was barely any movement, mostly because cars were trying to change lanes rather than move forward. Night quickly fell. While Maricar and Mariann deeply slept in the backseat, Erlat entertained the other girls with gossip, as Lu just stared out the window.

It did not take long until some more adventurous drivers decided to beat the traffic by going parallel to the highway in the sandy ground next to the road. We all watched as one after the other, these 4x4 cars of all shapes and colours cruised by in the desert. A few normal cars followed them and for a moment, I wondered if we should do the same and try to get home sooner. When Rizalino started to laugh, we all looked at him in curiosity. He gestured out the passenger window to an area where a pair of headlights were pointing upwards.

'Hahaha! Another one stuck in the sand! That will teach them a lesson,' he said with a smirk on his face.

Lu came out of her trance and looked at the white Toyota as two men got out of it, yelling at each other.

'Isn't it obvious to them that having a standard open differential would cause this?' said Lu.

We all stared at her, wondering which planet she had just arrived from. I was the first one to let out a "What?" before she continued.

'You need a differential lock, like the ones the 4x4s have, which forces both the left and right wheels on the same axle to always rotate at the same speed, regardless of tractional differences, so each wheel can apply as much rotational force as the traction under it will allow, and the torques on each side-shaft will be different. And a differential for the front and back wheels, too. That Toyota has an open differential, which always provides the same torque.'

Maricar giggled, Mariann clapped, and Erlat just stared. Jenny, Grace, Honorata, and I had our jaws dropped in amusement and shock. Lu looked at us and tried one more explanation: 'Unequal torque, equal rotational speeds!'

Everybody laughed, except for Rizalino, who let out a big "Wow!" from the front seat. Lu looked puzzled, so I jumped over Honorata and gave Lu a big, long hug. She smiled at me and said in a soft, almost embarrassed voice, 'Too many years helping Cereneo sell cars.'

I had already known it. And now everybody else knew it, too: Lu had a lot more to her than just beauty.

# 8

## ROOF ESCAPADES

There is always a time in our lives when we must say goodbye. Sometimes, we say goodbye all the time. And that was precisely how I felt: I had said far too many goodbyes.

It started last month, saying goodbye to Lu's joyful personality. She had not been the same since the night I found her crying in the dark living room, and she still had not told me what happened. Every time I asked, she claimed it was nothing and she had sorted it out already, or she simply did not want to talk about it. When I pushed her for an explanation, she used the "best friend" card, and lectured me on how best friends respect each other's privacy and silence. By now, I had stopped asking, but I surely missed the old, happy Lu.

The days were becoming very hot, and we knew summer had arrived, even though the calendar said it was still spring. Jenny, Erlat, Grace, and I even performed a little dance for the occasion, wherein we would go around in circles singing folk songs. Mariann lost no time in throwing a bucket of water on our heads and claiming we were doing a rain dance. Mariann could be mean and borderline evil sometimes, but we just laughed and enjoyed the refreshment.

We also said farewell to Grace, my cousin. She had completed her two-year contract and renegotiated only for another year. She had saved enough money to buy a little house back home and felt that her parents were getting old and it was time for her to settle down. Grace was twenty-eight and had started getting afraid that she was too old to find a good husband. Grace's departure was very difficult for me. She was family and I knew she would be there for me, no matter what happened. The evening after she left, I could not sleep, thinking of the sudden emptiness in my heart. Since I arrived, I had not spent too much time with her, as I quickly made friends with Lu and Honorata, but she was always there, looking after me at home or in the van, and I already missed her. When she left, she took many gifts for my aunt and uncle and a long letter I wrote to my father, who was happy, living a slow-paced life, and I wanted to reassure him that I was doing well.

Lu and Maricar were supposed to be going home with Grace, but they renewed their contracts for two more years.

Two days after Grace left, we threw a party in the evening to celebrate their stay. We invited the neighbours from the building and Honorata agreed to use her previous experience working in a bakery to teach us how to make cakes and cookies for the event. The men from apartment 341 brought the drinks and Rizalino collected the cooking ingredients during the day, so we had all we needed when we got back home. The following day was a day off for most of us, so we would be able to party until late.

On the day of the party, when my alarm rang at ten past five in the morning, I jumped out of bed, very excited about the evening to come. It was rare to have a mixed-gender gathering, and I had heard that the cute guy from apartment 205 would come. I'd had a crush on him for over three months now, but I still did not know his name. He was taller than me but skinny and looked to be about twenty-five years old. We had exchanged glances a few times when entering or leaving the building but apart from that, there had been no exchange of words or information. Lu and Grace knew nothing about him and I was too shy to ask anyone else.

Just as I was getting dressed, Erlat came to me and dragged me to a corner, where Jenny was waiting.

'Hi, Aubrey,' Erlat said with a smile and I could see she was plotting something.

'Uh... hi.'

'We have a proposal for you,' Erlat continued. 'We got an outside job that pays really well. It is only for today and we had it all agreed among the two of us, plus Grace. But now that Grace is gone, we are one person short. Do you want in?'

'But today is not my day off.'

'Neither is mine,' Erlat continued. 'We can just call in sick... say we ate something bad yesterday and are throwing up.'

'That is a lie!' I responded incredulously.

'Of course it is. Listen we have done this before, back in February. Wasim does not even check on us, so long as we show up the next day. He may reduce your salary by one day, but you will make five times that today, so it is worth it.'

'I don't know...'

'Listen,' Jenny interrupted. 'Your cousin would come with us. She is the one who arranged the job in the first place. It is safe, just a gardening job, actually easier than the cleaning jobs we normally do. It is in a big villa, where there will be a party tomorrow and they need the garden and patio areas to be impeccable. We will be cleaning plants most of the time, polishing the leaves until they are shiny and green.'

'Do they pay immediately?' I asked.

'On the spot. Cash. No questions asked.'

'And what if Wasim comes looking for us?'

'He will not. We can always say we went to the pharmacy when he came by.'

'Don't worry!' added Erlat, now holding my arm. 'We need you.'

'Five times my salary? I am not sure it is worth it,' I said.

'Come on, Erlat,' Jenny chided Erlat. 'Make it fair!'

'Okay, okay,' said Erlat, a bit disappointed with Jenny. 'Instead of the forty-five dirhams you will get for a day, they pay two hundred and eighty! And if we are lucky, there will be tips, so the total pay for the day can be up to three hundred dirhams. Are you in or not?'

I felt very uncomfortable with the deal, but the idea of extra cash and an earlier return home was very appealing. I guess my expression must have changed, because Jenny jumped on me and hugged me, saying 'thank you' a dozen times.

It was Jenny's day off anyway, so she just went back to bed, while Erlat coached me on what I should say to convince the others I was sick. As the other women in my room started to wake up, I stayed in bed, moaning a little bit and claiming that I had a stomachache. Time was so precious in the morning that most of them just ignored me, so they would not be late. Maricar was the only one who checked on me, and after putting her hand on my forehead to make sure I did not have a fever, she looked at me, winked, and told me to be careful. She obviously knew the scheme but did not seem fussed about the idea. It did not take long before they all went downstairs and boarded the van. Immediately, Erlat, Jenny, and I started to get ready and in less than ten minutes, we were dressed and ready to go. We walked down the road and waved at a taxi, which stopped almost fifty meters ahead, forcing us to run in its direction in the heat of the morning. Erlat gave the driver the address and off we went.

'This taxi will cost a fortune,' I muttered to Jenny.

'Don't worry. The transport is reimbursed; we just show the receipt and they pay us back. Erlat has the money for the fare.'

As we arrived at the address, my jaw dropped. The place was not a normal villa. It was a mansion, a palace. Erlat told us it was the residence of a European ambassador. I was not sure, as Erlat lied about almost everything, but the mansion was surely grand and very beautiful. We were greeted by a man who looked like a proper butler, in a dark grey suit and impeccable white gloves. He showed us to the back entrance and guided us through the smaller garden until we reached the larger garden and swimming pool area. It was beautiful! There was a lush green carpet of grass surrounded by white pebbles all around the perimeter of the property. On the left was a swimming pool bigger than the one in the club back home, rectangular, culminating in a waterfall. Palm trees were scattered around, just as plentiful as the crimson lounge chairs.

'You have four hours to finish this area,' the butler said. 'All the materials you may need are in that corner. I want all the chairs and stretchers cleaned and piled inside the garage.' He pointed left to another building.

'The bar at the end must be cleaned, as well as the patio leading to the house. The wooden floor has to be polished,' he continued. 'I do not want to see a speck of dust on any plant around here. And no chitchat with the pool cleaner. Hop, hop, off you go!'

He clapped his hands twice and waved us towards the corner of the garden where the cleaning products were. Erlat started to walk and took the role of team leader immediately, distributing the tasks amongst the three of us. As the morning came and went, so did a number of different professionals, from pool cleaners to gardeners and drivers. At noon, the butler came by and gave us something to eat. We had a fifteen-minute break and moved on to clean the smaller garden and the entrance of the house. The afternoon was busy with waiters, flower arrangements, and sparkling silver balloons that were placed in the swimming pool, making the water look like mercury. Several tables were set in the main garden and by the time we finished our work, we saw a group of musicians coming in, carrying their instruments in cases.

As expected, we got a large tip and that made the experience even more rewarding. As we sat in the taxi going back home, I prayed that we would not get in trouble with Wasim.

We arrived at the accommodation before the others and quickly went to the kitchen to help Honorata with the cooking. The house smelled like vanilla and, despite our begging, Honorata did not allow us to taste her amazingly delicious-looking cookies. I showered and put on a pretty white dress with small pink flowers on the hem of the skirt. I put on perfume and a little makeup and tied my hair in a ponytail high upon my head, which I thought could make my face look thinner. I never really liked my chubby cheeks and dimples, so I hoped that pulling my hair up would slim them down.

Around eight o'clock, the others arrived and Maricar was fast in spotting me and smiling.

'Looks like you are feeling better!' she chuckled.

'Much better!' I answered, winking back at her.

'You look so pretty. I hope he comes tonight,' she said.

I froze. How did she know? Was I that obvious? Had I overdone the dressing up? Maricar was surely very intuitive and I had to be thankful for her discretion, as she said nothing else that could potentially embarrass me.

By the time the guests started to arrive, the house was already bubbling with life. We closed the bedroom doors and placed the dining table against the wall, so people could move freely around the house. At one point, someone decided to leave the front door open, as the doorbell was getting annoying, ringing every two minutes. The news of the party travelled fast and before we knew it, there were over fifty people at our house. No longer fitting in the apartment, the party extended into the corridor of the building, which in turn attracted even more people. Some brought food, others brought drinks, and the atmosphere was great. I positioned myself strategically against the wall at the end of the living room, so I had a panoramic view of the kitchen, living room, and halfway through the corridor.

Hours went by and still no sign of my guy. Lu noticed my apprehension and calmed me down during the first two hours. After that, she lost her patience and started wandering around, looking for him. She decided to ask some of the other guys at the party, hoping they would know who she was talking about. Just as I was refilling my paper cup, Lu walked towards me, accompanied by an average-sized, broad-shouldered man in jeans and a striped shirt.

'Aubrey, this is Sunil,' Lu said, introducing the man next to her.

'Hi,' I replied shyly.

'He is a friend of Marvan,' Lu added.

I still did not understand and shrugged, hoping she would just spit it out.

'Marvan... from apartment 205!'

'Ah...'

'You see, Sunil,' Lu said, looking at the confused guy. 'My friend Aubrey found a bracelet on the steps the other day and she thought it belonged to your friend. We were hoping he would come by tonight, so he could identify whether it is his.'

'Sorry, but he is not coming.'

'Why?' Lu enquired, almost too abruptly. Sunil immediately looked suspicious, wondering what could have caused such an intense reaction.

Lu noticed her mistake and tried to correct it. 'Really, why? It would have been lovely to meet all our neighbours.'

She smiled and held her breath, waiting for Sunil to say something and break the strangeness in the air.

'Oh, Marvan had a date tonight.'

Lu and I looked at each other and we both said to Sunil at the same time, 'Date?'

'Yep. The guy is a flirt. He plays the innocent type, but he is probably the most creative person I have ever seen when it comes to meeting girls. Almost the opposite of me. If it wasn't for Lu approaching me in the corridor, I would probably not have spoken to a single person all night long.'

I was repulsed. I had never liked anyone before and the first guy I fell for was a womanising, serial-dating maniac. Never mind that he was creative. Creativity probably came hand-in-hand with infidelity.

'How creative, exactly?' Lu asked.

'Oh, I should not talk about it. Sorry, I am just nervous.'

'Why nervous?' Lu enquired, touching Sunil's arm at the elbow.

Sunil lifted his head and looked at me with a gentle, yet penetrating look that made me feel uncomfortable. I was curious to know about Marvan but something inside me felt it was not a good idea. Nevertheless, Lu was obviously more skilled at chitchatting and before I could end the conversation, she was already halfway through her speech about how we would be great friends now that we knew each other, and so on.

Sunil felt more comfortable, pulled out a chair, and explained the creative nature of his friend.

'I've known Marvan for three years now. We came in the same group hired to work as twenty-four-hour on-call electricians for a hotel chain. The money is good and despite having to work twelve hour shifts every day of the week, most of the time, we just sit around waiting for something to break down. The shifts are from six to six and...'

'Six to six what?' asked Lu, extremely interested in the story.

'Six in the morning to six in the evening, or six in the evening to six in the morning. When I arrive at work, he goes home, and vice-versa.'

'So, you never see each other?' I asked.

'Well... we do meet for quick handovers at work and often, one of us stays a bit longer to chat. This way, we save on rent, paying only half because we share the same bed. So, continuing with Marvan's story...'

I could see that Sunil was enjoying the attention and I saw Lu smiling for the first time in many months. However, instead of feeling happy for her, I found myself consumed with a strange feeling, one of anger and perhaps jealousy. Sunil continued, 'Marvan has this *routine* where he approaches some of the girls who come to the hotel,' he said, winking at Lu when he said the word *routine*.

'He picks up the guests?' I asked incredulously.

'No. Not the guests. The servants, usually nannies who come with their employers to spend the day at the beach club. During the week, the Madams usually sit by the beach getting a tan while the nannies are in the kid's pool or the kid's club, looking after the children. Because Marvan works the shift of six in the morning to six in the evening, he gets to see them all day long and monitor those who are frequent club members. When he sees a girl that he likes, which are most of the girls anyway, he sneaks out of the maintenance room with the excuse to check the pool pump system, carries his radio with him in case the hotel reception calls with an urgent job, and approaches the nanny he fancies. He is a smooth talker and somehow, he always finds out where they live.

'He only goes for girls living in Dubai.' Sunil paused, making sure we were still interested in his story.

'This is where his plan gets creative. If the girl works and lives in a villa in the Jumeirah or Umm Suqeim districts, he proceeds with the plan. If they live in an apartment or in a villa somewhere further away, he chats a little more and presses a button on the radio, which makes a ringing sound. He then pretends it is an emergency call and goes away without hurting anybody's feelings.'

'Why does he pick those two areas?' Lu asked.

'Wait and you'll see,' Sunil replied, creating suspense. 'Marvan would propose to meet the girl before his work starts, around four in the morning, and she would undoubtedly answer that she could not. Employers normally kept a close eye on their maids, so she most likely slept in the child's room and she was definitely not allowed to leave the house, apart from on her day off. She would probably also complain that she could not use her mobile phone, especially in the very early morning hours that Marvan proposed. Initially, it would sound like an impossible case, but this is where the benefit of choosing girls who live in a villa comes in. He would ask for her address and tell her to find out what type of roof the villa had, and how she can get access to it. You will be surprise by how easy it is to climb to the top of some villas, as their roofs are not made of the inclined ceramic tiles we are used to. They are flat or semi-flat concrete tops, more designed to protect from the heat than the rain.

'The next day,' he continued, 'or the next time the girl came to the club, Marwan would ask specifics about the roof and ascertain whether it was a feasible option or not. Most of the time, it was, especially the older villas in Jumeirah and Umm Suqeim. Those neighbourhoods were also not too far away from the hotel and Marvan would use the maintenance bicycle to go there and back to the hotel, the trip being at a maximum twenty-minutes long. So, assuming the girl had come back and told Marvan that she could get to the roof relatively easily, he would give her a portable flashlight, a card with simplified Morse code signs, and a small, vibrating alarm clock, and agree to meet her at four in the morning the next day. The girls loved the idea of secrecy and adventure and felt very encouraged by the fact that they would not have to leave the house to meet him.'

'But wouldn't it be so much easier to just use the mobile phone flashlight and alarm apps? This makes no sense!' Lu said, exasperated.

'Well, the girls loved the objects Marvan gave them and saw them as a firm commitment that he would show up and that he trusted them. The trust worked both ways, as Marvan exploited their trust and commitment to the maximum on the first date. The girl would go home, do her duties, and at night, she would set the alarm clock for three-thirty, put it under her pillow, and go to sleep as usual. When the alarm vibrated, without waking up the children or the other maids or nannies in the room, she would sneak out and go to the roof of the villa. By that time, Marvan would have gotten there on the main bus, which comes to the hotel for the cleaners' shift, which starts at four o'clock. While I was still on duty, he would get the maintenance bicycle and cycle to the girl's house. If anyone at the hotel needed me, I just walked or got one of the golf carts, which between four and six in the morning, were never used anyway.'

'Oh, so you help him out, don't you?' I said, smiling at him without realizing it.

'Yeah, well... I don't endorse his actions, but he is a friend, after all.' He paused and looked a bit embarrassed. 'So, Marvan would arrive at the girl's villa and search for a safe location outside where he could see the roof of the villa where the girl lives. Then he would flash his flashlight and wait for a response. When the girl saw the signal, she would use the paper card he gave her with the simplified variation of Morse code to signal back *okay* or *not okay*. There have been occasions when the child was sick, and the nanny could not stay away for a long time, and she had signalled *not okay* and then signalled another day of the week for a new meeting. Assuming the signal was positive, Marvan would go to the roof of the girl's villa.'

'How did he get there?' Lu asked.

'Most roofs can be accessed from a ladder on the outside of the villa.'

'But he is trespassing! Surely that is illegal!' Lu gasped.

'I've told him a million times, but he doesn't listen,' Sunil added, ashamed.

'Then what happens?' I asked.

'I am embarrassed to talk about that. Let's just say they would get to know each other extremely well. The warm weather, gazing at the sky, and watching the dawn break can be very romantic indeed.'

Sunil was blushing; his eyes had a glow of a long-lost, pleasant memory. Even though the story was entertaining, it was also infuriating to learn that the guy whom I had hoped to meet could be such a calculating and meticulous person when it came to dates.

'Did he ever get caught?' I asked.

'No. But he tends to stick to the same girl for a while, as long as their sexual exchanges pay out for the flashlight investment.' Sunil laughed but I noticed that only one side of his mouth lifted.

'What a pervert!' said Lu, punching him in the upper arm.

Sunil looked at me and our eyes locked in what seemed to be an eternity. There was something magnetic yet pure in him, which made me forget why we were asking about his roommate in the first place. Clearly, Marvan was not who I thought, but Sunil was shy and funny at the same time, and quite an interesting guy.

Lu cleared her throat. 'Sorry to break up this moment...'

Sunil and I stirred from the trance connecting us and we both looked embarrassed about what had just happened. He quickly moved two feet away and offered to get us drinks. Lu accepted and offered to go to the kitchen with him when he turned around and asked me, 'So where is the bracelet you said you had? I can show it to Marvan and ask if it is his, if you want.'

'Um, never mind. You can ask Marvan anyway, but I doubt it is his. I will just keep it until someone comes to get it back,' I lied, not sure I convinced Sunil at all.

'By the way,' I added, 'how come you were able to come to the party? I thought you worked the night shift?'

'I called in sick and asked someone to replace me today. I knew about the party and there was a person I really wanted to meet here.'

Sunil lowered his head and Lu and I looked at each other in disbelief. Could that person be one of us? Before I could muster the courage to ask him, Lu and Sunil had already disappeared among the masses of people standing the living room. I thought it was funny that he'd used the same excuse as I had that day. I'd made more money, but he was after something more personal. Maybe that person was Lu, or maybe it was me.

As I remained in the corner of the living room, alone, I had mental conversations with myself, thinking about how odd it was that even though I was celebrating Lu and Maricar staying in Dubai, at least for another year, I was also saying farewell to the idea of Marvan. I recalled the English book I was studying back in the Philippines almost a year ago:

> *Farewell is what you say to someone whom you don't expect to see again, meaning, 'may you fare well'. Goodbye, which is derived from 'God by ye' - God be with you - is to be said when you leave someone, even if you may see him again very soon.*

Marvan and his roof escapades were definitely gone from my plans. As I celebrated one year in this new country, I hoped my path would cross with Sunil's again. Preferably very soon.

# SUMMER – 2009

# 9

## COMING CLEAN

*Sunil, Sunil...* I caught myself daydreaming about the skinny, introspective guy a lot these past few days. The summer was passing by rather quickly, and I could not remember a single thing that happened in July, apart from Sunil being in my thoughts and seeing Lu back in good spirits.

The scalding forty-five-to-fifty degrees Celsius was usually enough to boil a person's brain at midday, and I often prayed and thanked God for giving me a mostly indoor job and an accommodation with air conditioning.

Wasim had been less stingy and allowed Rizalino to have the air conditioning in the van switched on at full power on the way back home. Going into work, the weather was less hot, and he claimed there was no need for such extravagance. I felt lucky, as every day, I saw the white buses with the brand Ashok Leyland on the back, carrying men from the construction sites back home to the labour camps. The men were cramped inside, never an empty seat available, all windows opened, and about a dozen little plastic fans spinning from right to left, blowing hot air into their faces. They either slept leaning on each other's shoulders or lively chatted with smiles on their faces. Blessed should be their resilience and blessed was my luck to be in a van with air conditioning.

One day the previous week, Wasim came with us in the van after work for a surprise inspection of our living conditions. He spent over one hour in the front seat, next to Rizalino, talking about cleaning standards and a potential governmental check, which he wanted the firm to pass with high marks. The only problem was that, for the entire journey, the van's air conditioning blew the cold air filled with the smell of Wasim's sweat into our nostrils. It was repulsive. How could he preach about cleanliness if he could not keep his body in a condition which was not harmful to others around him? Only God knew what sort of fungus was growing underneath Wasim's armpits!

The inspection went well, but all we could talk about afterwards was the nauseating smell. Honorata claimed it was his diet, full of spices, such as cardamom, cumin, turmeric, chili, and coriander, but the consensus was that he just needed a good scrub in the shower.

It was on the evening of the inspection that Lu opened up to me with surprising revelations. I had stopped asking about her troubles a long time ago, as she insisted it was nothing and just cried at night. A few times, I woke up in the middle of the night to find her staring out the window, sobbing, with a tissue box secured in one of her hands. I would go over to her and give her a hug until she had calmed down. I would then go back to bed and we never spoke about it the following morning.

The day we met Sunil at the farewell party, almost two months ago, was the first day I saw Lu smiling naturally. She slowly became less depressed and as we bumped into Sunil in the corridor, her moods started to lift. Over the summer, we had fallen into a routine of meeting up with Honorata, Sunil, and one of his friends every Monday night, which was Sunil's day off. The five of us walked around the block and often just sat at the corner of our street, chatting and drinking colas. Monday became my favourite day of the week, and many times, I caught Sunil staring at me. I would blush and look away, only to glimpse at him again, casually, a few seconds later. Sunil's friend seemed nice and we all just gelled together like a group of old school friends. Sometimes we even forgot the guys were not Filipinos and we naturally switched from English to Tagalog without noticing, and they would stare at us, not understanding a single word of what was going on.

During the entire month of July, I only saw Lu crying once. I rejoiced at the idea that whatever was bothering her would be going away for good soon. I'd been patient and knew that sooner or later, Lu would need to talk to someone. It happened on Wasim's inspection day.

'Hey, Aubrey,' Lu whispered. 'Let's go downstairs. I need to talk to you.'

'Now?' I replied, surprised. 'It is my turn to do the dishes today. Mariann will eat me alive if I sneak out now.'

'Okay, okay. Finish up and we will talk then. Please?'

Lu had a way of getting people to do what she wanted. When she said *please*, she made a puppy face, lowering her face until her chin almost touched her chest and then raising her eyelids, so all one could see was her penetrating pair of eyes, enchanting the subject of her plea.

I rushed through the dishes and Mariann praised me for the speedy work. That should have been the first sign that the evening was not going to be a usual one, as Mariann never praised anyone. She was mostly too grumpy to even say 'good morning' and lashed out at us over any mistake. No wonder she was divorced. A man would have to be a masochist to withstand a relationship with her.

I put the apron on the kitchen counter and found Lu standing outside the door, impatiently waiting for me.

'What can be so important for you to be stalking me during dishes time?'

'I have been unfair to you, Aubrey, and I just realised it today,' Lu said, her eyes filling up with tears.

'Oh, c'mon. Don't cry... please. I am your friend. Don't be upset because of me.'

'But I've been so foolish. You are my best friend and I've kept so much from you.'

Lu paused and wiped her face with the tissue she had in her pocket.

'Let's go downstairs so we can talk,' she said, grabbing my upper arm.

We walked through the corridor and down the stairs in silence and my mind went a million miles per hour, imagining what was going on. What was her secret? Why did she decide to tell me now? Was it over?

We stopped at our usual spot in the parking lot, where two walls were joined together in an L shape, all the way at the back of the building. We could see the people coming and going from the front of the building, but they could not hear us, as it was a quiet place, away from the street and the heat from the main ventilation system. We moved the cardboards which were leaning against the wall, shook them a little to take the dust off, and sat down on the floor cross-legged, looking at each other.

'I am indebted to you, Aubrey,' Lu said.

'Stop it!'

'No, I really mean it. You have been an amazing friend. More than I could ever have hoped for. You saw me suffering and looked after me but did not ask me for an explanation.'

'I was only keeping my promise to you. You asked me not to ask again and so I didn't.'

'I know... and this is what makes you such a good friend. I was talking to Sunil today and he mentioned how patient and insightful you are and...'

Lu was still speaking but I had stopped listening. Did she really say Sunil was talking about me? And saying good things? My heart was racing so fast I could hardly contain my excitement.

'Aubrey, are you listening to me?' Lu prompted.

'Um? Ah, yes, yes. Sorry, I got distracted. You were saying something about Sunil?'

'No, I was saying something about *you*. About who you are. Although, I could talk about Sunil for hours.' She winked at me and my fists tightened. It was an involuntary reflex and I hoped Lu did not notice it.

Did she like Sunil, too? I would never be able to compete with her looks and charm. And how come she was talking to Sunil today? Did they spend time on the phone regularly?

'So, I was saying that you have been very patient and tolerant of my crying and moaning. I feel more at peace with myself now, and I think it is only fair that I tell you the reason for my odd behaviour over the last few months.'

'Ah... okay.' I shrugged, nodding and trying not to sound too excited.

'Do you remember Angelo?'

'Angelo... your ex-fiancé? The one who married a senator's daughter while saying he was in love with you?'

'Yep! That's the one. To me, he has been dead and buried, away from my mind since the day I landed here.'

'I know. That bastard! Trust me, if I ever meet him, I will make sure he is dead and buried for real!'

I punched my leg in a sign of forcefulness and decisiveness but did not realise it would hurt. My face contorted, and I let a loud scream out, which made Lu giggle.

'So, you can imagine my surprise when, one day, my phone rang and guess who was on the other side of the line?'

'Angelo? No!' I shouted.

'Yes, him. The first thing I did was shout some obscene words at him, which my mother, God rest her soul, would be ashamed to hear. I told him to never call me again. And just before I hung up, he said: *Wait, I am in Dubai.*'

My face turned white. I was in shock but also dying of curiosity to know what had happened next.

'I was speechless,' Lu said, a little embarrassed. 'I wasn't sure if he was serious or joking, and he caught me by surprise with that statement. He wasted no time in asking me to be patient and give him just a minute, so he could explain himself. I agreed to give him two minutes and looked at my watch as he went on. At the end of two minutes, I wasn't able to interrupt him. His story was compelling and explained so many things that had happened during the days we were together.

'Angelo told me he knew I was saving money from the car and clothes sales and he thought I expected a better quality of life by being with him. Despite having a job, his salary was not much, so he engaged in some illicit ventures with one of the senators to diverge funds from a telecommunications contract into a private account in Angelo's name. After a couple of weeks, Angelo would clean this money, sort of like money laundering, investing in properties abroad and registering them in someone else's name, usually the senator or one of his children. Angelo would keep ten percent of the transaction value for agreeing to have the initial account in his name and doing some paperwork here and there for the senator.'

'Ten percent does not sound like much, given the risk he was taking,' I interrupted.

'You are wrong! It was a lot of money. It would not only be enough to buy the beach hut Angelo had promised me when he took me on the honeymoon weekend, it would be enough to buy the entire island! They were transferring massive amounts into his account.'

Lu's eyes were full of tears, her nose red and puffy. I held her hand tight but said nothing, waiting for her to catch her breath and finish the story.

'But then, one day, a reporter investigating scandals and corruption in the higher levels of the senate found out about this specific senator's fortune and started digging for evidence. She knew something was wrong but could not pinpoint the source of the money. She was clever and so, pretending to be just another girl in a bar, she befriended Angelo, hoping he would spill the story. She did not know he was involved and only hoped he would give her a hint, so she could continue her investigation. Angelo, being who he is, tried to impress her by buying expensive bottles of champagne and inviting her out for dinner in one of the chicest restaurants in Manila. She got suspicious, did some digging around on Angelo, and found out about his ever-growing bank account. When they met for dinner, she had printouts of his bank statements and a voice recorder ready to capture all his explanations.'

'Oh my God!' I said. 'This guy is worse than I imagined. Before, he was just an ass for leaving you and marrying someone worthy of his career ambition. But now, he is a crook and a criminal!

'Ah, my friend,' Lu continued. 'You don't know the half of it.' She tried to smile with tears in her eyes, as if revealing the true Angelo was both painful and satisfying. She continued, 'When Angelo met the undercover reporter for dinner, she came clean to him about her identity and threatened to disclose the scam. She promised to hide Angelo's identity if he agreed to expose all the senator's illicit transactions. Angelo told me on the phone that he freaked out and thought about suicide or running away to Indonesia. But being a crook meant he had the skill of being a quick thinker and he played her, using his incredible charm, asking her for five days so he could gather the proper information before coming clean. The restaurant they were at was very upscale and had a spacious dining area with tables far apart from each other. She felt it was the perfect venue to discuss private matters and dine on his expense, so they agreed to meet again in the same place in five days' time.'

'Haha. At last, a woman taking advantage of Angelo! I like that,' I said with a huge smile on my face.

Lu raised both eyebrows and looked at the floor, the same look a card player would give when they knew their hand would not win them any points. I had a hard time understanding Lu. Why was she upset? If Angelo was in trouble, she should have been happy. But then, why did he come to Dubai looking for her?

'Angelo went immediately to the senator and told him the entire story,' Lu continued. 'The senator was an influential man, powerful and with connections both on the political and the underground, criminal level. The senator's first reaction was to make accusations and blame it all on Angelo, saying he talked too much and was careless with his show-off attitude. But Angelo knew that as long as his neck was on the line, so was the senator's, as he would have a lot more to lose if Angelo talked. They spent two days locked in the senator's office, fighting and discussing, only having contact with the outside world when the delivery man came with some food. Exhausted and in need of a shower, both men shook hands and sealed a deal to solve their common problem.'

'What was it?' I asked impatiently.

'It happened that the senator's daughter had always had a crush on Angelo. She wasn't particularly beautiful, and her horrible temperament had driven away many suitors over the last ten years, so she found herself past the ideal age to be married. Her father was afraid that any man marrying her would only be interested in either his money or his political influence. The senator also knew that his daughter was a liability to his political career if she remained unmarried. Hence, he decided to offer his daughter's hand in marriage to Angelo. Making Angelo part of the family would certainly buy his silence. In exchange, the senator offered to take care of the journalist, increase Angelo's share in the profits from ten to twenty percent, and allocate the properties already in his daughter's name to Angelo. That meant a house in Switzerland

and two large plots of land in Thailand. The money spoke higher than his love for me and he agreed to the proposal. At least, this was Angelo's explanation for why he, all of a sudden, was getting married to a senator's daughter who was fifteen years older than him.'

'But the journalist? She would go on with the story, right?' I asked.

'The senator also promised to *take care* of her and Angelo believed the senator would be using his power to get her transferred to another newspaper or even to another country.'

'Wow!' I answered in shock. 'That almost sounds too complicated to be true. Did you believe him?'

'At that moment on the phone, I did not, but the more I thought about it, the more it made sense. Angelo did say I was his true love and that would explain his marriage to such a woman.'

'Yes, but the excuse that he was stealing money just to give you a better life is bullshit!' I vented at once. 'The man either has morals and principles or he doesn't! Besides, you don't come across as a woman who needs an island to be happy.'

We both laughed, stretching our legs over the cardboard boxes on the floor.

'So, what did Angelo want with you, then?' I asked.

'He was running away. After the wedding, everything settled, and the bride seemed to be as pleased with the arrangement as her father. As part of the dowry, Angelo got a nice house on the outskirts of Manila and a significant lump sum to buy furniture and a new car. He told me he did not love the senator's daughter and when I asked him about their marital bedroom, he said he was obliged to perform in bed but that it was a mechanical act in which he always fantasised about me.'

I looked at Lu in disbelief.

'I know, I know!' she continued. 'I almost fell for it, but the scars he left were deeper than any sweet talk he could throw at me. Anyway, despite his claims, he said he was fairly content with the way things had worked out. He did not hear from the reporter again and assumed everything was taken care of.'

'Why was he running away, then?'

'He would not say over the phone but wanted to meet me in person to explain himself. He said he came to Dubai to get me, so we could run away together. I could not believe my ears! At first, I thought he was lying and was calling from the Philippines, as the call sounded distant and full of interference. But he proposed to meet up in a few days, so he could explain everything in detail and agree on a date to fly back to the Philippines together. He did not let me speak much and hung up the phone just after telling me the place and time we should meet.'

'Did you go?' I asked incredulously.

'Yes,' she answered immediately, in a nonchalant manner.

'Oh my God! Were you crazy?' I snapped at her.

'I knew you would be upset. This is why I didn't tell you.'

'Sorry.' I paused, looking embarrassed. I tried to swallow my fury. 'So, what happened?'

'I am not an idiot, Aubrey. I confided in Maricar. I told her the entire story and she, like you, felt it was a mistake to meet him. But, she offered some help and asked Rizalino to go with me, so he could assess what was going on and make sure

I was safe. On the following Sunday, I asked Wasim to only assign me an afternoon job, claiming I was not feeling very well that morning. Wasim can be a pain sometimes but there are advantages to being his protégé and enduring his tasteless comments. Just before lunchtime, Rizalino took me to the large parking lot in front of the Co-op Supermarket and there he was, dressed in an expensive-looking suit, wearing aviator sunglasses, and holding a small black suitcase. I almost didn't recognise him, as he looked more like a mafia man than the guy I once fell in love with.

'Rizalino,' she continued, 'parked the van and got out first, which made Angelo apprehensive. For every step Rizalino took in his direction, Angelo would take a step back, until I got out of the car and both men stopped where they were and just looked at me. I signalled to Rizalino to stay put and went towards Angelo. Angelo came towards me and made a gesture, as if he was going to hug me, but I stepped aside and made sure there was an arm's-length distance between us at all times. He started to mumble but I was very direct and asked him to explain exactly what kind of trouble he was involved in. He said that about a month earlier, the senator asked him to make a money collection at one of the real estate firms they frequently dealt with. The senator insisted on Angelo taking a bodyguard with him – in particular, Jose, who was the senator's personal bodyguard. They arrived at the office and were pressuring one of the top executives for some money he owed to the senator, when a group of security guards started to push Angelo and Jose out of the building. Things turned bad, shots were fired, and before Angelo realised it, Jose had the executive's body hanging across his shoulders and was running down the corridor. Angelo claimed that the only thing he could have done was follow Jose. When the bodyguard dropped the executive into the trunk of the car, Angelo entered through the passenger door and asked no questions, still too shaken by what had just happened. Jose drove for almost twenty minutes and parked inside a warehouse with a large container-style office in the back. The place looked abandoned and Angelo made no move to get out of the vehicle. Jose opened the warehouse door and walked in, as if looking for something. Then he kicked the ground a few times, bent over, grabbed a flat hinge from the floor, and opened a trap door, leading to an underground area. Jose went back to the car, opened the trunk, got the executive's dead body out, and walked back inside the warehouse. Angelo followed Jose with his eyes through the car's side mirror until Jose started going down the steps. Angelo, not containing his curiosity, got out of the car and followed Jose. The trapdoor was open, and Angelo went downstairs, quietly, touching the dirt walls, trying to get his eyes adapted to the darkness. A few rays of light passed through the underground roof and Angelo noticed there were other hatches and that the underground area was just a hole in the ground, pure soil, no finishing on the floor or walls at all. About fifteen meters ahead of him, a flashlight went on and Jose started to shout at Angelo for not waiting in the car. Jose grabbed Angelo's arm, dragged him to the end of the tunnel, and placed a shovel in Angelo's hand.

'*I want to see some dirt moving,* commanded Jose, his brow covered in sweat. Both men started to dig up the soil on the right and deposit it to the left corner of the narrow hall, where the body of the executive lay, full of blood, facedown on the ground. Angelo complained and said they should call the doctor, but Jose wasted no time in threatening Angelo, claiming he now was an accomplice, and bullying him to dig faster. Angelo took two steps back and just stood there, watching the executive's body being submerged in soil.

'By then, Angelo's eyes were accustomed to the low light underground. He mastered all the courage in the world and told Jose he would not help him anymore, but he would not talk, either. He said he just needed to get out of the tunnel and that he would be waiting in the car for Jose. Angelo walked towards the pile of soil and dropped the shovel on the ground and as he was preparing to turn towards the exit, he saw a hole in the ground with a shiny piece of metal sticking out. Jose was too busy digging and did not notice when Angelo took the shiny name tag out of the ground and read the name on it. It belonged to the reporter who was investigating his involvement with the senator months before. Angelo saw that a piece of cloth was hanging from the name tag and as he pulled it up, a decomposed hand popped out of the ground. Angelo, in shock, ran as fast as he could, entered the car, and drove off at high speed, not bothering to wait for Jose or even close the trunk.'

'The reporter was dead!' I exclaimed, feeling like I was watching a suspense movie.

'Yes,' Lu continued. 'And Angelo believed the senator *took care* of the issue by having her killed. Angelo felt sick, stopped to throw up, and continued to drive until he reached his house. His wife was waiting for him, asking him what was going on, as her father had called three times already, looking for him. Angelo knew it was just a matter of time until Jose told the senator about Angelo's discovery, so he told his wife he had an urgent meeting he needed to attend to, went to his office, opened the safe, took as much money as he could fit in his briefcase, put his passport in his jacket pocket, and stormed out of the house. He claimed he took the first plane out to Malaysia and then got a connection in Qatar. He landed in Dubai the day he called me.'

I was speechless. I thought these kinds of things only happened in movies and here I was, listening to my best friend in complete astonishment.

'Do you really think he came just to get you?' I asked in disbelief.

'At first, that is what I thought. But after telling me the story, he went on and on about his bank accounts being blocked by the senator, how he was running out of money, and that he had paid a fortune for the last-minute airline tickets. He claimed he could not go back to that sordid world, especially now that he found out that the senator was involved in more than just some corruption here and there. The senator was an assassin and would undoubtedly drag Angelo into that side of his business.'

'Yeah, but too late to want to jump out of the boat now, hm?' I interrupted, blood boiling in my veins.

'Too late or not, Angelo was interested in getting help, both financially and in the form of a new name and passport. So, he came to me, begging me to take him back, saying he loved me and that he had made a mistake. He also asked for ten thousand dollars. I must have been in shock, because I involuntarily started to walk backwards, away from Angelo. Rizalino noticed and honked the horn of the van, signalling that we had to go. Luckily, I recovered my senses and told Angelo that I would meet him again after three days, at the same place. I would bring him the money and a contact person who could provide him with a new identity.'

'No. How could you, Lu?'

'Calm down, calm down. Maricar was very clever and she foresaw that Angelo would ask me for money at some stage. She very carefully instructed me to agree to his demands, pretend to be interested in whatever he offered, and then ask for some time. This way, I could report back to her and decide what would be the best action plan. I wanted revenge for all the pain Angelo caused me and this could be the perfect opportunity to get it. Being emotionally involved did not help and Maricar was a good, rational sounding board for whatever I wanted to do. So, after much discussion, we decided to turn Angelo in to the police, but we would need some evidence, or at least a confession from him, telling the story again. Rizalino was very helpful in contacting the authorities, given that he had already met some of the people in the police department during Belinda's robbery case. His one condition was that he would not get involved and would only be a conduit, so I could speak to the right people at the police station. A senior officer met me the following day and guided me through the process of convicting Angelo, which would involve a recording device attached to my chest, an undercover policeman pretending to be a passport counterfeiter, and a disguised police vehicle with video cameras hidden in strategic places to record every move. You can imagine how tense and nervous I was, dealing with the police and having to face Angelo again. I hope you will forgive me for my erratic behaviour during that period, Aubrey.'

'I am the one feeling bad, Lu,' I said. 'There I was, thinking you were just depressed, when in fact, you were going through all of this mess!'

I moved closer to Lu and gave her a tight hug. We stood there in silence for a while. Some people passed by on their way to the stairs and looked at us in an inquisitive way. We did not care what others would think of two girls hugging in the dark corner of the parking lot. I was just happy to have my friend back.

'Did you go ahead with the police's plan, then?' I asked, pulling away and looking into Lu's eyes.

'Yes, on the day I had agreed to meet Angelo, Wasim had to give me the day off, based on a police order. I went with all of you in the van to work in the morning, so no one would suspect anything. The police were very adamant that the entire plan, or *operation*, as they called it, remained a secret. Maricar, Rizalino, and I had to sign many documents saying we could not talk about the operation until one month after Angelo had been deported.

'On that day,' she continued, 'after Rizalino dropped everybody off, he took me to the police station, where the preparations for the meeting with Angelo begun. Two female officers briefed me and secured a wireless microphone inside my blouse. We roleplayed a few scenarios, like if Angelo tried to get more intimate or if he discovered it was a set-up. They told me to be relaxed and friendly but act reluctantly in taking Angelo back. This way, he would have to explain himself in more detail and hopefully, the police would catch it all on tape.

'At two o'clock,' she continued, 'I was sitting inside the police officer's car at the Co-op parking lot, waiting for Angelo to show up. The car was a common, white, off-road Toyota and the policeman looked as dodgy as one would imagine a criminal might look: unshaven, dark glasses, cotton shirt tucked in, and brown trousers. The policeman was sitting in the driver's seat and I was next to him. He had a gun under his seat and another one attached to the side of his seat, so it would be easier to reach. When Angelo arrived by taxi, the policeman told me to go meet him and convince him to go to the car in order to talk to the passport counterfeiter. I got out of the car and walked towards Angelo, who seemed very happy to see me. He looked into my eyes and gave me a hug, which caught me by surprise. His smell made me sick and I pushed him away, telling him that this kind of demonstration of affection was not allowed in this country. He pulled back and joked that he would not want to get in trouble with the local police. His comment made my heart skip a beat. I kept looking around, trying to see if any of the undercover policemen had appeared. I was obviously nervous, and Angelo told me it was a joke, that there were no police around and we were fine. I tried to smile and told him that I had managed to borrow some money from friends and in total, I had more than the sum he had asked for, and that I found a man who could help with his new identification.

'I moved towards him, held his hand, mine covered in sweat, and walked towards the white car. I opened the back door and jumped in, making a gesture for him to get in the front. Angelo entered the car and shook hands with the policeman. *I hear you are in trouble*, said the policeman. *Yep and I need some new documents*, said Angelo. *Can you help?* The policeman answered: *Possibly. But I need to know who I am dealing with and what kind of trouble you are involved in.* Angelo's face turned harsh, his teeth grinding, lips tight and sparks seeming to come from his eyes. *I don't think you need to know anything*, Angelo said. *The situation is very simple, I have money and you have a passport. It's a pure exchange.*

'The policeman asked him how quickly he needed the documents, and Angelo said he needed them by the next day, to which the policeman announced that it would cost more to get them so quickly. Angelo asked how much more, and the policeman told him it would cost fifteen thousand dollars. Angelo was outraged. *This is insane!* He shouted, his face turning red. *I can get new passports in the Philippines for two thousand dollars!* To which the officer calmly replied: *Then go back to the Philippines to get your new documents.*

'A strange silence fell upon us in the car and I thought I could hear my own heart beating,' Lu continued, her hands trembling. 'Angelo asked the man if he could talk to me alone for a while. The policeman agreed and volunteered to step out of the car and grab a coffee at the kiosk nearby while Angelo and I talked inside the air-conditioned car. This was a perfect set-up for the cameras and also because Angelo could not run away easily. Angelo asked how much money I had with me exactly and I said sixty thousand dirhams, which was just over sixteen thousand dollars. He looked pleased and asked me to hand it over to him but I had been instructed to make him talk before showing him any money, so I told him that the last time we met, it was all very confusing to me, and that the story he had told me was full of gaps and I needed him to explain to me again what had happened.'

Lu paused and made sure I was still listening.

'I guess he was so desperate for the money that he didn't mind going through the story again. I kept interrupting him with specific questions, such as how he knew it was the journalist's body and where exactly the warehouse was located. Angelo talked fast, and we must have stayed there for about forty minutes when he started to get nervous about the fact that the passport man was nowhere to be seen. He thought something was odd, and that such a person would not just sit there and wait forever like this. Angelo looked around once more and told me we should step out of the car and I should give him the bag with the money immediately. I reached for the door handle with my right hand while my left hand held the bag containing the money between the two front seats. I quickly told him I would go look for the man, got out of the car, and walked towards the kiosk. The policeman was walking out, certainly having listened in on our conversation, since it had been recorded by the microphones. As we passed each other, he smiled at me and nodded positively. I felt an immense relief and walked even faster towards the cafe where the two policewomen, dressed in their abayas as a disguise, were waiting for me. One of them held me by the shoulders and said I did really well. She explained that all they needed now was for Angelo to proceed with the illegal passport purchase, so he could be arrested immediately. Five minutes after I had entered the café, I saw a group of policemen in uniforms running towards the car, dragging Angelo out and handcuffing him.'

'Why are you crying, Lu?' I asked as tears rolled down her cheeks.

'I know I should have been happy to see the crook being arrested and finally getting my revenge, but deep down inside, I was suffering. I once fell in love with Angelo and although he had become a different person, I felt that maybe he did not deserve this. Maybe his punishment should have been to remain married to the old, ugly senator's daughter, doing dirty work here and there. But I also felt relief, as if the burden of a broken heart had been lifted from my shoulders.'

'So, what happened to Angelo?' I asked.

'He got arrested,' Lu explained, 'and the authorities in the UAE made an agreement to deport him to the Philippines, where he was going to remain in custody and be charged with corruption, extortion, and murder. They said his sentence would be reduced depending on how much information he gave about the senator's involvement, but he was expected to spend enough time in jail to never bother thinking of me again.'

'And you could not say any of this to me?'

'I had to sign the police agreement. I could not share this with anyone, as the investigation was still going on in the Philippines. I am dying to tell my brothers. Can you imagine how happy Carlo is going to be?'

Lu was smiling; it was a fresh smile I had not seen for a long, long time.

'How can you be so brave? You are such an inspiration,' I said, proud of my friend.

'You are stronger than your think, Aubrey,' she said, looking me in the eye. 'We have to stand up for ourselves and not let the oddities of life take us down. We have to be in control of our destiny.' That last phrase echoed in my mind several times, challenging my beliefs and making me wonder if I would have done the same if I were in Lu's shoes.

We looked at our watches almost simultaneously and saw that it was past two in the morning and we would have to wake up in a few hours to go to work. I wasn't tired and wanted to ask Lu a million questions about the last two months. She agreed, still smiling.

'Let's go upstairs,' she said. 'Everybody should be asleep by now and we can talk in the living room.'

I nodded, and we walked upstairs, hand in hand. The next three hours flew by and the Angelo story entertained my curiosity for a few more weeks.

Lu said it was good to be able to talk and not hold secrets back. To come clean to her best friend. How ironic that, in that same evening, Wasim had come to inspect the cleanliness of our accommodation.

# 10

# FORBIDDEN ADVENTURES

Almost a month had passed since Lu told me the Angelo story. Our friendship was back to normal and so was Lu's emotional state. No more crying at night or dark circles under her eyes. The weekend before, I had gone with her to buy a phone card and listened to her conversation with her brothers. At one point, she stopped talking and I could hear a group of men on the other side, cheering and screaming, as if they were watching their favourite football team score a winning goal. Carlo was so ecstatic that he promised to attend all the court sessions for Angelo and visit him in jail, just to make the criminal's life miserable. Lu became a heroine in their eyes and one of her brothers, Crisanto, asked her if she got any reward from the police. She did not get anything; the sixteen thousand dollars which she showed to Angelo in the car went back to where it had come from: the police. She said she got her peace of mind and two days off from work, courtesy of the police through a legal order directly addressed to Wasim. Lu was happy and that was all that mattered.

Our evening encounters once a week with Sunil and his friend continued We were happy that soon, summer would be over, and the weather would be more pleasant for hanging out outside. Marvan, the womaniser, never joined us and I suspected it was on purpose, as Sunil felt embarrassed by his friend's behaviour. Some other people would join us every now and then. Jenny was becoming a regular and a much-welcomed addition to the group. Erlat, on the other hand, would invite herself, despite our attempts to sneak out without her noticing. She could be difficult sometimes, and we knew she was a compulsive liar, so it was always unclear which one of her crazy stories were really true. But she was funny, and Sunil's friend seemed to enjoy her company.

One evening, when coming back home, Erlat interrupted an interesting conversation Lu and I were having about Sunil and what type of women we thought he fancied. We didn't say it out loud but both of us knew too well we were talking about ourselves and trying to guess if he would be interested in either of us.

'If Sunil saw a tall, slim, and beautiful girl in the mall, he would definitely approach her,' I said, teasing Lu.

'I don't think so,' Lu responded. 'He would prefer a calmer, more intellectual girl, someone he can talk to for hours and hours. The beautiful type only attracts men for the first date. The nice type has a better chance in the long run.'

We would laugh and tap each other on the shoulders. It was evident that we both had a crush on him, despite his unusual appearance and different nationality. Maricar once told us she had no idea what we saw in Sunil. She thought he was too skinny, dressed like her grandfather, and had the voice of a twelve-year-old boy. She never spent any time with him to know the kind, centred, and mature guy he really was. His looks were deceiving, and we knew that despite having a fragile body type, he also had strong hands and the agility to fight or run a marathon. It was in the midst of our conversation that Erlat interrupted.

'Guess what, girls?' Erlat said.

'What? You won the lottery? You are going back home? You kissed Wasim?' Lu said in a sequence, annoyed by Erlat's sudden appearance.

'Gross!' Erlat said, twisting her face. 'I can do with the money and a trip home but do not mix pleasure with Wasim's image, please!'

We all giggled.

'I've got something new. A new toy.'

'A toy?' I asked.

'Not just any toy, silly!' Erlat answered. 'A *forbidden* toy.'

'Like what?'

'You know... one of those... *intimate* toys.' Erlat was grinning from ear to ear.

Lu and I looked at each other, puzzled.

'You mean a sex toy?' Lu asked, without blushing.

Erlat nodded and shook her bag, signalling something very secret was inside.

To me, it was a big taboo to talk about sex, especially if one was not married. I was brought up as a strict Catholic, going to mass every Sunday and confessing at least once a month. My mother insisted that I complete my religious studies and perform my first communion by the age of eight, and I had my confirmation immediately after I had my first period. To remain a virgin until marriage was something I had never questioned, and I knew nothing different until I came to Dubai and met Lu. Often, I would catch Maricar and Mariann talking about some gynaecological problem, but no one ever dared to explicitly talk about their sexual adventures or fantasies with me. It was obvious to me that many of the girls in the compound had already had sexual experiences, including Lu, but none of them bragged about their forbidden encounters. Well... none except Erlat. She always had a story about a friend of a friend who did something naughty somewhere. She seemed too knowledgeable in many aspects, from marital relations to adultery to foreplay and now, obviously, sex toys.

  The conversations with Erlat were usually one-sided, with her doing most of the talking and us rarely asking questions. It was difficult to say how much of it she was making up, but she often quoted a magazine called *Cosmo* as her source. She said that before she came to Dubai, she used to work at a beauty salon, where they subscribed to a few foreign magazines, as most clients were expatriated women. *Cosmopolitan*, or *Cosmo* as she called it, was a magazine which often answered readers' sexual dilemmas and had pages and pages of articles about pretty much every taboo subject.

  Erlat also claimed she already had several experiences in the field, but I somehow doubted her. I could not believe someone with her figure and personality could attract any suitor. Maybe I was being mean, and I should know better not to judge people, but she was four times the size of Sunil and since the very first day we met on the airplane coming to Dubai, something did not settle well between us. Maybe it was the way she looked at me after I was molested in the plane's toilet, or perhaps I was just jealous of her knowledge about things and her romantic stories.

'So, are you going to show us the toy or not?' asked Lu.

'Soon. Are you going out tonight? I can come and show you then,' she said, winking.

'No way!' I objected. 'The guys are going to be there, and I am not looking at anything in front of them.'

'Fine, fine,' Erlat said.

'We are not cooking today. Why don't we meet at the stairs just before dinner?' proposed Lu.

'Okay,' Erlat confirmed. 'We can go to the stairs leading to the garage. It should be quiet there.'

Our building was unusual in that the garage occupied the first floor of the building but could only be accessed by either the car ramp or a separate set of stairs. The main staircase connecting the ground floor entrance to all the other floors occupied by apartments was separate and did not lead to the garage. Most people in the building did not have a car, so the garage was often empty, and its staircase was seldom used. The staircase was narrow with two ninety-degree bends and the walls, painted light yellow many years ago, were in desperate need of a fresh coat of paint or at least some cleaning.

We arrived home at seven-thirty, and fifteen minutes later, Erlat whistled to grab my attention and signalled towards the door. I tapped Lu on her shoulder and we walked out of the apartment. Lu, Erlat, and I went to the ground floor and exited to the street level, just to re-enter through a small metal door next to the main entrance. We walked up a few steps, passed the first turn on the stairs, and sat down. This way, no one could see us either from above or below. We would certainly hear if someone were to open the door and that would give us time to stand up and leave in the opposite direction.

Erlat looked nervous and made us swear to never tell anyone about what we were about to see. At first, I did not understand why Erlat was so secretive about her object. She later explained that it was part of a number of prohibited items in this country. In general, pornography was not allowed at all, including movies, magazines, books, and obviously, sex toys. She said that even sculptures or artistic paintings that did not adhere to the religious and moral values of the country were forbidden. We all knew of the normal customs of many countries, such as a limit on quantities of cigarettes or alcohol, and forbidden items, such as firearms and drugs. In Dubai, they made it explicit that ivory items were prohibited, as well as counterfeit currency. Radioactive substances were also prohibited and although I was sure this was the case in many other countries, I sarcastically thought that these last two rules must have restricted business with the neighbouring Iran.

Erlat was laughing when she explained these restrictions and joked about items, such as gambling chips, telescopic lenses, and laser pens, being confiscated at the airport. She said that if the police at the airport were to enforce the law, they would have to arrest every tourist with a camera and every lecturer with a PowerPoint slide and laser pointer. As usual, I could not tell if Erlat was telling the truth or if she had made up this list of prohibited items, but I was convinced that the pornographic items were not allowed and that was enough to make me apprehensive about what she was about to show us.

Erlat carefully opened her handbag and took out a round package, poorly wrapped in brown paper. She handled it with care, as if it was some fragile and very precious artefact, and started to unwrap it gently, so as not to damage the wrapping paper. To me, it took an eternity, but I held my comments in order not to appear anxious or too curious. When the paper was lying flat on Erlat's lap, she lifted the conical, pink item as if it was the Holy Grail. We all gasped. It looked like it was made of rubber and had a small opening at the bottom for the insertion of batteries to make it vibrate.

'How did you get it, Erlat?' I asked.

'Remember, you promised never to tell anyone,' she warned us.

We nodded our heads in agreement.

'I've been cleaning the same house for a few weeks now, and until last week, the house was sparsely furnished. The couple who lived there had moved to Dubai, but their belongings were still in a container being shipped from England. I easily moved the few pieces of furniture around to clean in the corners because the drawers and closets were empty. Then, last week, their shipment arrived, and I had to move the dressing table next to the main bed in order to clean behind it. With the movement, the top drawer slid open and a few objects became visible.'

Erlat's eyes were wide open and she continued in a reticent voice.

'They had so many toys: silicon rings, cylindrical vibrators, all sorts of lubricant gels, and even some items which looked like a part of the human body.'

'You mean...' Lu stopped, searching for the words. 'It looked like... a man's part?'

'Mm-hm.' Erlat nodded, grinning.

'And you went ahead and took one? Are you insane?' I asked, more in shock with the fact that she had stolen something than the object itself.

'There were so many items and they were all in a big mess inside the drawer. I doubt they will notice something was missing.' Erlat paused. 'Even if they do, no one will say anything. Can you imagine the Madam calling Wasim to say her vibrator went missing?'

She was right. I could not imagine it, but I was revolted by her attitude. It was one thing to fake a sick day, but to steal was something else entirely. She should have known better after the repercussions from Belinda's case.

'What are you going to do with it?' Lu asked.

'I hope you don't plan to use it, Erlat!' I shouted. 'I sleep in the same room as you and I don't care if you want to keep this a secret. I will not be in the same room as you when you... oh, this is gross!'

'Calm down, pure Cinderella!' Erlat was laughing so hard she choked and started to cough convulsively.

She took a long breath, cleared her throat, and continued. 'I will sell it, of course. Do you have any idea how much an item like this will fetch on the black market? The English couple got lucky because their things came in a large shipment and I doubt people check every box. But I can get almost fifty dollars for this. It is brand-new. And looks very high-tech.'

'So, you'll risk your job, being deported, humiliation, and going to prison, all for fifty dollars?' Lu said, indignant.

'It's for the thrill of it. The adventure,' Erlat said, winking at Lu.

She barely finished saying the word *adventure* when we heard the door below us opening. Erlat panicked and stuffed the vibrator into the white plastic bag she was holding and put the brown paper on top, all wrinkled up, to cover the object inside. She stepped behind Lu just before a man appeared at the corner of the stairs.

'Sunil! You almost killed me!' Erlat said, her face red and covered in sweat. 'I can have a heart attack with you sneaking around like that!'

'All I did was walk upstairs. I do not know why you are so worked up,' Sunil answered.

We looked guiltily at each other and I had made up my mind that I would not be the first one to talk.

'What are you doing here, anyway?' he asked.

'Girl stuff,' Erlat responded abruptly. 'None of your business.'

'Okay, okay, I was just looking for you girls because I know we are meeting later tonight and I wanted to bring two friends, so I came to ask if it was okay with you.'

'That is very considerate of you, Sunil,' I said. 'It would be odd if it was just Lu and me and a bunch of guys around us.'

'Problem solved, then,' Erlat interrupted. 'I will come with you and balance the gender problem.'

Lu and I looked at each other and nodded in agreement.

'Let's get moving, then,' Lu said. 'Dinner must be ready.'

'I just need to go down to the trash room and throw this package away,' Erlat said, shaking the plastic bag. 'I will meet you girls upstairs.'

'Please, let me be a gentleman,' Sunil said, quickly grabbing the plastic bag out of Erlat's hands. 'I am going downstairs anyway to get us some drinks. I can throw this in the building's master bin.'

Sunil moved hurriedly downstairs, his skinny fingers tying a knot with the handles of the plastic bag. Erlat was frozen, not sure how she possibly could run after him and insist she would take the bag herself without causing suspicion. Just a second later, we heard the door slam shut behind Sunil, and he was gone.

'What am I going to do?' Erlat panicked.

'Why did you say you were going to throw it in the trash?'

'I couldn't go back upstairs with the thing unwrapped. I thought I would go to the trash room and wrap it properly so the others at home would not get curious or see it by accident!'

'Ha, ha. You wanted adventure?' Lu said, an evil smile on her face. 'Good luck digging in those large bins, full of trash.'

'You have to help me,' she begged Lu.

Lu shook her head, still smiling at Erlat's disgrace.

'Aubrey, please? With my shape, I will never be able to climb the tall sides of the bin.'

'I am so sorry, Erlat. But fifty dollars is not enough and the only adventures I am interested in are adventures of the heart.'

Lu and I walked upstairs, leaving Erlat to contemplate her options for recovery.

Almost an hour later, she arrived at the apartment. We had finished eating and were getting ready to go downstairs to meet Sunil and his friends. Erlat passed through the living room quickly and went straight to the bathroom. Everybody noticed the stinky smell of trash she left behind when she passed. I was certain she'd had enough adventure for the evening.

**AUTUMN – 2009**

# 11

## IT'S A DOG'S LIFE

The thing I loved about October was that, for those who had been here a while, there was a noticeable change in the weather. Not only had it cooled down by a few degrees but the attitude of people on the streets also changed. It also got cooler. It was as if the population decided to chill and enjoy life a bit more.

To no surprise, the number of events in town started to grow and social life became busy with just a turn of the calendar page. It was difficult to say which was the cause and which was the effect, but the fact was that, no matter what social class you belonged to, there was always something interesting happening the moment October started.

Last evening, over dinner, Jenny came with a full list of events happening in town during the next two months. There were concerts, theatre shows, and exclusive parties at the beach, all of them requiring a significant financial investment which none of us were prepared to put up. But there were also some free activities, such as fireworks by the creek, art exhibitions, and movies on a rooftop. The one which caught my attention was a competition in the old district of Satwa. It would be held in two weeks' time and the registration deadline was in two days. It required teams of people who were willing to prove their skills in ironing. The participants would be divided not by gender or age, but by the type of garment to be ironed. There was the men's shirt category, abayas, t-shirts, and even a bed linen category. Anyone of any nationality could enrol, so long as they were over eighteen years old, had authorisation from their employer, agreed to be responsible for any damaged garments during the competition, and competed in no more than two categories.

After spending so much time together, Jenny, Lu, and I had reached a stage where sometimes, words were not necessary, and our glances already exchanged the brainwaves needed for a full conversation.

'Mm-hm,' Lu nodded at the same time as Jenny.

We laughed, as we knew our ironing skills were unmatchable.

'Who is going to ask Wasim for a day off?' I asked.

Jenny and I were looking at Lu, as we knew she was going to be elected for that task anyway. We offered to do all of Wasim's laundry the next month, in exchange for the shift in the work schedule. He would not suffer, as all he had to do was rearrange the days so Maricar and Erlat would work instead of us on that day. If Lu used her charm well, it could work.

'But you only have until tomorrow to convince him and get the authorization letters,' Jenny said.

'Okay, okay. I feel the pressure already,' Lu responded, short-tempered.

'Which categories are we signing up for?' Jenny asked.

'I definitely suggest the bed linen. Our teamwork on holding and folding will be great!' I said.

'Let's just avoid the abayas,' Lu added. 'Although they are all black, the different fabrics mean different temperatures and there is always one made of satin or some other delicate material which needs to be ironed from the inside out, so it doesn't leave marks.'

I giggled and remembered the first time I went to do a cleaning job for an Arab woman and she asked me to iron her abayas and her husband's dishdashas. I looked at her, a question mark stamped across my face. What were those things? Inevitably, I found out they referred to the long black robes the women wore and the white robes for the men. They seemed like an easy task, but I quickly discovered how challenging it was to iron a black abaya full of embroidery and little sparkling stones attached to it. They might be black, but the Arab women here certainly knew how to embellish them with the most beautiful floral and geometric designs. That day, I looked forward to the men's garments, noticing they were plain with just two inside pockets at thigh-height. Made of the softest cotton, these garments, called *thaub* or *kandura* by the locals, or dishdashas by us, were a spotless white and need to be extremely well-pressed. Once, not happy with the way I had ironed her husband's dishdasha, the Madam gave me a lesson on the amount of starch I should use on them. All I can say is that the manufacturers of Merino starch should be very happy with their clients in Dubai, for when I finished the load of ironing, six bottles had been used and the dishdashas were so firm and rigid that I could probably have used them as wall partitions in my bedroom.

That night, we went to bed with high hopes for a weekend in Satwa.

The next two weeks passed by very quickly.

On the day of the event, we woke up at five in the morning to prepare ourselves. The competition did not start until nine-thirty, but we wanted to get there in time to get used to the equipment. We agreed to take the van to work and then take a taxi from there, as it would be a short ride and we were confident that the prize money of three hundred dollars per category would offset any investment in transportation.

Wasim had agreed to let all three of us have the day off at the same time but renegotiated with Lu that his laundry would be done for two full months and that Lu would be the one collecting and delivering it to his office. At first, I got scared by that part, wondering if Wasim would be molesting Lu on those occasions, but she assured me that he was all talk and no harm, and just wanted an excuse to stare at her in private.

We had a brief breakfast and boarded the van towards the main office. From there, we headed off to Satwa by taxi. The competition was going to take place on one of the side streets, where many of the tailoring shops were located. Satwa could be delimitated by three main streets, two of which ran parallel to each other and had a small block between them which hosted mainly parking lots, a few shops, and the main Mosque of the area, an imposing and beautiful sandy-coloured building which filled up during Friday prayers. The ironing competition was on one little street two blocks away.

I liked to call the third main street in Satwa *flora-and-fauna street* because of the shops selling plants, vegetables, and animals. I had to admit that most of the shops on this street sold fabric for garments, as well as upholstery and curtains, but the fauna shops were my favourite.

On the day of the competition, we arrived too early for the event, and after registering at the main desk, we had almost two hours to spare before our category would be competing. So, Lu, Jenny, and I went for a walk along the streets of Satwa. This was really a city-inside-a-city. All the smells and sights were so different from any other part of Dubai. The tiny shop which held only one man inside serving Pakistani street food competed for attention with the large gift shop that sold pretty much everything you could imagine. The items were not sophisticated, and many were, in fact, bad quality, made-in-China types of items, but the prices were very reasonable, even for me and my low salary.

We headed towards flora-and-fauna street and decided to explore it, from beginning to end, entering and exiting the stores at leisure. The first place we went in was a supermarket which contained a department store. The concept was a strange one as, in most cases, it was the other way around. On the second floor, just as we exited the escalator, there were a multitude of products made in Japan that were both cheap and very amusing. All three of us decided to buy a sombrero-type hat for one dollar each, just for fun, keeping a souvenir from our adventurous day out.

We continued to go in and out of shops until my favourite pet shop arrived. They had all sorts of different fish, turtles, hamsters, rabbits, and birds. The impressive scarlet macaw was so beautiful that I was tempted to ask the man behind the counter for the price.

'No, Ma'am. We cannot sell this bird,' he told me, apologetically.

How nice it was to be called *Ma'am* for once! For more than a year, I had used the word Ma'am or Madam so many times that hearing it directed at me was a shock.

'Ma'am,' the man called me. 'Are you okay? I am sorry, I cannot sell you the bird.'

'Why?' I asked him.

'This is a pet macaw. These animals are protected, and it is illegal to sell them.'

'Really?' Jenny asked. 'I thought all one had to do was to go to Southeast Asia and just grab them. I am sure they are abundant there!'

'All I can tell you,' he continued, 'is that in this country, it is illegal to sell them.'

Funny, how he did not agree nor disagree with Jenny's comment and I wondered how he got the animal here in the first place, given that it was illegal.

'What about dogs?' Lu inquired. 'Don't you have any puppies?'

The man was now losing his patience and just said, "No dogs, no dogs," shaking his head and looking busy. I knew many people in Dubai considered dogs to be dirty animals, or *haram* as they say, meaning impure or sinful animals. In my mind, I could not imagine a creature of God being sinful just for existing. But I suspected that the combination of a very hot summer and the lack of places to walk the animals put many people off.

We walked out of the store, noticing how we made the salesman uncomfortable with our questioning and our lack of intention to actually buy anything. We must have moved thirty meters along the road when a Filipino woman touched my shoulder from behind. I stopped immediately and turned around, only to see Danda with her arms open, ready to hug me.

Danda was an old friend from the Philippines. We met when she came to visit some relatives in my hometown. I was about ten years old and although she lived far away, we always kept in touch through letters and we would see each other every couple of years during the school holidays. I had not seen or spoken to Danda since my mother passed away and therefore had no idea she was also living in Dubai.

'Holy baby Jesus! Danda!'

'Aubrey!'

We hugged for the longest time.

'What are you doing here?' she asked.

'I work here... for more than a year now,' I answered.

'You never told me you were coming. I've been here for two years.'

'I am sorry... I lost touch with you. I went through a difficult phase; my mother passed away and my plans for college went downhill. So, I came over to do some cleaning, save money, and hopefully change my life once and for all.'

'Oh, Aubrey. I am so sorry about your mother!'

She hugged me again, tapping me on the back.

'What about you? What are you doing here?' I asked.

'I work as a secretary for an Indian businessman. In fact, I am more of a personal assistant, as I do pretty much everything around the office. Typing, answering the phone, serving coffee, paying the bills, chasing customers. You name it and I do it.'

'A secretary job... sounds great! How did you get the job?'

'When I was at university back home, I saw an advert for skilled women interested in secretarial jobs. They needed someone who could type, speak good English and Arabic, and was willing to work hard. The salary was very good, and I thought I would give it a try. So, I asked the university to hold my place for a year and came over.'

'I didn't know you spoke Arabic.'

'Well, at the time, I was not fluent. I asked a friend of mine who spoke very good Arabic to pretend she was me on the phone interview. I quickly realised that the employer was not an Arab himself and spoke a very limited amount of words in that language. Therefore, in the five weeks between getting the job and coming over, all I did was study Arabic. When I got here, the contract was signed, and it would cost my boss a lot of money to send me back, so he kept me employed with the agreement that I would study Arabic in my free time. He made the right decision, as I am good with languages and in six months, I was answering the phone for customer complaints.'

'I am impressed! You taught yourself Arabic?'

'No, not really. You know what they say: The best way to learn a language is to get a lover. So, I did. My relationship with a Palestinian man did not last, but surely my Arabic became much, much better.' She smiled.

There was so much I would have loved to hear from Danda, but I felt that questioning her about her personal relationships would not be wise, given that we just gotten back in touch after so many years.

'How much longer are you staying? Are you going back soon?' I asked.

'No. I just renewed my contract. I decided to stay. Life here is good; I live in the maid's quarters in my boss' house, in a nice part of town. I pay no rent and save in one year what it would take me seven back home.'

'I see. It's so good to see you again. By the way, these are my friends, Lu and Jenny. We live and work together.'

'Hi. Nice to meet you,' they all said, almost at the same time.

'I am glad you recognised me,' I said.

'I was in the pet store when one of you asked about dogs. This is one of the lines of business my boss is in. He sells dogs and I wanted to warn you about getting them.'

'No, no. I am not interested in getting a dog,' Lu quickly answered. 'I was just curious. I don't have a place to put my toothbrush nowadays, how could I possibly have a dog?'

'Just in case, if any of you know someone wanting a dog, just let me know. There are three ways people go about getting a purebred puppy in this country. One is to go to the pet shops, who will charge you up to six thousand dollars for a dog. Most people think this is a lot of money to pay for a pet and they start looking on the internet. And here is where the scams start. There are countless gangs from Nigeria, the Congo, and Cameroon who will send pictures of pedigreed puppies and will promise to get the animal to you within forty-eight hours. Their price is usually very cheap, around five hundred dollars, but they ask for an initial deposit to pay for the airline costs. That is when the client wires them the money and never hears from the seller again.

'I know of a client,' Danda continued, 'whose sellers told her they were based in Manchester, England, but gave her a telephone number in Cameroon. She later told me that the people on the phone had heavy accents and the money transfer was sent to Cameroon, but they assured her that this was only to avoid taxes. She paid three hundred dollars and got nothing in return. When I asked her if she checked how they were going to send the animal, she said they would send it by air on the next direct plane from Manchester to Dubai. That flight route did not even exist, and this shows you how people can be easily fooled.'

'So how do you sell the dogs?' I asked.

'My boss has good contacts with breeders from Thailand and Ukraine. He has been in Dubai for many decades and has fostered good relationships with some key agents at a smaller airport in the UAE. Once the client has specified what type of animal he wants, my boss makes a phone call to the breeder and the selected animal is put in a cage and dispatched on the next cargo plane over here. Either the driver or I go to pick the animal up. We make sure the relationship with customs and immigration agents remain sweet, if you know what I mean, and bring the animal to the office. My boss then delivers the animal for less than two thousand dollars to the client.'

'Is this legal?' Jenny asked.

'Clients only pay the money when they get the animal in their hands, so we have never had an unhappy customer. And we are the only ones who can, in fact, deliver puppies who are three months old.'

'How so?' Jenny asked, interested in the story.

'For the pet to enter the UAE, it needs to have all its vaccines in order, and there must have been thirty days since the last rabies shot was given. But the rabies shot can only be given to a puppy at the age of three months, so officially, no animal can enter the UAE before being four months old.'

'How do you do it, then?'

'The animal gets shipped between the age of two and three months, but the papers say the animal is four or five months old, with all the vaccines given.'

'They are fake papers?' Lu asked.

'For a quarter of the pet shop's price, you get the same dog, and just need to take it to the pet shop to get it vaccinated, which should not cost more than a hundred dollars anyway. So, all in all, the clients love it.'

We all looked at each other, thinking we would rather not know any more about the business of pet smuggling. We fell into silence and my mind was quickly thinking of ways to change the subject once and for all.

'Hm, you seem to be doing well in that business. Too bad the city is not very pet-friendly. By the way, did you hear about the new beach park opening in Jumeirah?' I said, hoping someone would start to talk about beaches and move on to another subject.

'Yes,' Danda answered, and I smiled, thinking my plan had worked. 'I know what you mean about it not being pet-friendly. Dogs are not allowed on beaches, inside any of the parks, or even in many of the buildings. In Islam, dogs are only allowed as working animals, such as a hunting dog or for protection, and Muslims should clean themselves after touching the animal if they are going to prayer. We explain to people that dogs are mentioned in the Quran in three passages, especially in the one about the cave people, the righteous ones, who stayed inside a cave for three hundred and nine years with their dog lying at the entrance of the cave, guarding them. When asked about how many people there were in the cave, the dog was always counted among them. This usually reminds people that dogs are creatures of God and should be treated with love, too.'

'I can see you became an Islamic scholar, Danda!' I said jokingly.

'It's all part of the sales pitch.' She winked at me.

'Oh, look, it's almost time for our category to start,' Lu said in a panicked voice.

'Sorry, we have to rush, Danda,' I added. 'We enrolled in the ironing competition, which starts in twenty minutes. What are you doing now? Do you want to come and watch us compete?'

'Sorry Aubrey, but I have to get going. But let's keep in touch. Here is my phone number,' she said, pulling a business card out of her purse. 'Where do you live?'

'In Sharjah,' I replied. 'Here is my number.'

I gave her a piece of napkin with my number written on it.

'Sharjah is far, but I really want to see you again.' Danda looked at me, her eyes filling up with tears. 'I feel I have let you down, not being there while you went through a hard time. There is a lot we need to catch up on. I want to hear all about you.'

Danda looked the same, but she surely talked a lot more now. Jenny and Lu were already moving away a few steps, and Lu was tapping her watch. Before I could suggest something, Danda continued. 'I will call you tonight and we can arrange a meeting for next week.'

We hugged again, and I ran towards Jenny and Lu, who let out little barks as soon as we were far away from Danda.

'What was that dog lecture all about?' Lu asked.

'It's your fault! You started it by asking the poor man at the shop for puppies!' I replied, laughing.

We reached the registration desk just in time to be allocated our workstation. The first category was dishdashas. The plan was for Jenny to operate the iron, Lu to place the garment on the ironing board in different positions, and I was supposed to spray the starch when needed.

There were another thirteen work stations and the teams varied from one person working alone to teams of five. We knew the single person would be at a disadvantage, but we were also puzzled by how five people would manage to synchronize activities without interfering with each other and becoming a liability. We found out the answer exactly twenty minutes later, as that was how long the competition lasted. The hanger next to our workstation was full, and we were assured that if we needed more garments, they would just magically appear on the hanger, although the record was thirty-five dishdashas.

The siren blared, and the clock started to tick. Chaos took over the area as people ran desperately, garments flying over their heads and steam bursting out of the industrial irons. Both of my hands were holding starch bottles and my index fingers were firing away, spraying starch like bullets in a cowboy movie.

Jenny tried to shout instructions to Lu, but the amount of noise from all the participants and the audience was so loud that they could not hear each other. I saw their lips moving but had no idea what they were saying. The steam from the iron made a hiss and indicated that the last drop of water had been used. How could we have been so careless and not bring water? Our workstation was a mess and I saw how other teams advanced much faster than us. Ten minutes into the competition, I glanced at a team with only two small ladies, positioned ten meters away from us. They did not speak a word and functioned like a machine, all synchronized. They already had twice as many dishdashas ironed than us. We did not stand a chance.

When the siren blared again, marking the end of twenty minutes, we dropped the iron, counted the garments on our hanger rack, and realised we had accomplished only a pathetic thirteen pieces. The winner was a team of four Indian men, all dressed in short-sleeved, light-blue outfits. They were smiling and posing for a photo next to a tall and beautiful woman with the thirty-two pieces they had ironed hanging behind them. In fact, they had done thirty-four, but two were rejected and disqualified due to wrinkles on the collars. That was it; the three-hundred-dollar prize moved out of our dreams and into the Indian men's hands.

It was not a surprise how this event was profitable. With an average of twelve teams per category and dishdashas being charged anywhere between ten to twenty dirhams per piece to be ironed by the laundry shops across town, the organizers could pay the prizes, make a profit, and still get free publicity from the event.

We had forty-five minutes to get ready for the next category in which we would be competing: bed linens. Jenny, frustrated by our embarrassing performance, devised a plan for us to perform like robots, not talking, all moves precisely executed to allow us to win this time. When the time to get set at our workstation came, we had exhaustively rehearsed the seven key moves of holding the bed linens, stretching and sliding them onto the ironing board, and counterintuitively to the normal way of ironing, we would have the iron itself fixed and the linen underneath it continuously moving. This way, the iron could be filled up constantly with water and steam would be pumped to the max without needing intervals to recharge.

This time, there were twenty-seven teams competing. It was the last category of the competition; the sun was high in the sky and I could feel droplets of sweat forming on my lower back.

'Get set, ready... bang!'

The clock started to tick, and it was like the three of us were in a trance. Arms moved in wave patterns, stretching, folding, and sliding. I did not hear any noise this time, but I was sure it was purely due to my complete focus on the task, isolating all noises and distractions. The twenty minutes flew by, and when the siren blared again, we froze holding a double bedsheet, light-yellow with flowers embroidered at the edges.

We folded that piece, knowing it would not be counted anyway, and placed it on the unfinished pile. It was only when the judge came and started to count the duvet covers and bedsheets that we noticed how our pile was significantly taller than the others. One by one, the pieces were counted, and points were awarded depending on the complexity of the item. Duvets earned the highest points and pillowcases earned the lowest points. We amassed a total of ninety-seven points and Jenny signed the sheet stating our overall score. We had to wait half an hour for the results and the announcement of the winners. The three of us sat at the curb, next to the main administration desk, where a big umbrella provided shade. Under the table, I spotted a fluffy, furry little thing moving inside a printed Louis Vuitton bag. The zipper was open and the head of the little dog popped out, its tongue hanging from its mouth, trying to cope with the heat.

'Look!' I told Lu, poking her in the ribs with my elbow. 'It's a dog.'

'Call it over here, let's see if it comes to us,' she replied.

'Tsk, tsk... doggy, come,' I ordered.

The dog climbed out of the bag, walked straight at me, and jumped onto my lap, wagging its tail frantically.

'And the winners from the linen category are...' announced the man holding the megaphone. '... Miss Aubrey, Miss Jenny, and Miss Lualhati.'

We looked at each other in disbelief. We had won! Jenny started to cry, her fat cheeks turning red. Lu stood up, jumping up and down like a child. I got up, too, and we all walked towards the man with the megaphone to receive our prize.

'I can see you made a new friend,' the man said to me.

'Gucci! There you are!' A tall, slim, and very beautiful woman with a high-pitched voice screamed from behind the man.

The pretty woman walked towards me and, with one hand, gave me a cheque for three hundred dollars, while the other hand stretched out, trying to reach the dog cuddled in my forearm.

'Oh, Ma'am. I am sorry,' I said. 'I got so excited about winning that I did not notice your dog was still in my arms.'

I handed the dog to her, while Jenny grabbed the cheque from the woman's hand.

'You can keep the money and the trophy but my Gucci-baby you can never have!' she said, patting the dog's head and covering the animal with kisses.

That afternoon, we took the bus home, the three of us very happy and a few dollars richer.

'What are you going to do with the prize?' Jenny asked.

'I need a new dress to go on a date with Sunil,' I said.

'What?' Lu asked, perplexed.

'He finally got the courage and asked me out. Just the two of us going out for a meal. I don't want to look like a rag on what might be a very important night of my life.'

'Congratulations,' Jenny said, hugging me.

Lu said nothing and looked away, through the window. I felt fearful of asking her why she seemed upset, as I already suspected that the answer involved her having feelings for Sunil, too. I deliberately did not expand on the details of the date, despite Jenny's insistence.

'What about you, Lu? What are you going to do with the money?' Jenny asked.

Lu looked at Jenny, paused for a few seconds, and said, 'I will buy a Gucci-printed dog collar, fake of course, and wear it as a bracelet to remind me that some dogs have a better life than I do.'

We all knew it was a joke, but there was some hard truth behind it.

*187    Zana Bonafe*

# WINTER – 2009

## 12

## THE PRICE OF INDEPENDENCE

We all had been waiting for Independence Day. Similar to the USA, where the Fourth of July is celebrated with much partying and fireworks, the second of December is also a big day for the Emiratis. Back in 1971, they peacefully obtained independence from Britain and formed a federation, today with seven Emirates. Most people knew about Dubai because of all the accolades it had received, from having the tallest building in the world to the biggest crisis in real estate. Abu Dhabi was known because it was the capital, but the other five emirates were mostly unknown outside the Arab world.

When I got recruited and was told I would be living in the Emirate of Sharjah, I first thought they had made a mistake. I had never heard of Sharjah and took me a good search on the internet to find out where it was. It was only when I arrived that I realised some of the Emirates were very small, and sometimes they were, in practical terms, just the city-next-door.

The best aspect of Independence Day was the fact that we did not work. Sunil had a last-minute call from his work on the day of our planned date, two weeks ago, and we were not able to meet. He had replanned the date as a daytime event on Independence Day, when we both would have time off. At first, I was very upset because not only was I not meeting him as soon as I had hoped but also the romance of an evening date was spoiled by a daytime event. He tried to convince me that we would have more time to talk and would be able to enjoy the fireworks together in the early evening.

On Independence Day, I woke up full of apprehension, hoping this would be the beginning of my dependence on him. I got dressed, ate breakfast quickly, and headed off to the Deira City Centre shopping mall, along with half the people from the apartment. We preferred this shopping mall over the large Dubai Mall or the glamorous Mall of the Emirates because it was closer to home and had a Carrefour supermarket. There was no point in window shopping at Zara and H&M, if at the end of the day, all we could afford were clothes from Carrefour. We could do our food shopping there, too and because there were so many other Filipino maids and Pakistani drivers, no one looked at us differently, thinking our Madams were two steps ahead of us.

I looked for a new dress or top to wear on my date with Sunil later that day. I remembered that Lu once told me that yellow matched my complexion and highlighted my dark hair, but I was not so sure if I should get something in that colour, as every person I saw wearing yellow either looked pale or as if they were wearing a uniform. I found nothing I liked and, at twelve o'clock, we headed back to the bus stop, bags with groceries in hand, to go back to our accommodation. I had not spoken about my date with Lu, as I suspected she was jealous. I never dared to ask if it was envy or jealousy, but in any case, I did not want to upset my best friend.

When we got home, Lu let me shower first and, as I walked out of the bathroom, Lu was waiting for me by the door.

'I prepared something for you,' she said. 'Come, come.'

She grabbed my hand and pulled me to her bedroom, where a beautiful dress was hanging from the side of the bunk bed.

'Wow! This is beautiful,' I commented.

'I want you to wear it today,' she added.

I was speechless. Did she know about my date? Why didn't she say anything before?

'It is really pretty... thanks. But... how do you know where I am going?'

'Oh, Aubrey! Do you really think these walls can keep secrets? Everyone knows about your *secret meeting* with Sunil. Here,' she said reaching for the dress and putting it into my arms. 'I want you to look stunning. He will not take his eyes off you.'

I quietly let out a 'thank you', unsure what else to say. I had lied to Lu and she was being so nice to me.

Our sizes were very similar, and her dress fit me perfectly. It was made of a light fabric, imitating silk, and the skirt fluttered rhythmically with every step I took. The small print in red-and-orange gave the white background of the fabric an incredible feeling of autumn while still being very feminine. I looked at myself in the mirror and felt extremely pretty.

I noticed a headband on Lu's bunkbed. The hairband was made of satin and had little orange flowers on the top. It would go nicely with the dress, and I took no time in asking Lu if I could borrow it.

At first, she looked shocked. Then she mumbled something about it not being a good idea. I insisted, and she reluctantly held the hairband, looked at it, and let out a sigh.

'I guess it will look nicer on you than on me,' she said sweetly. She removed the elastic band holding my hair in a ponytail and slid her fingers through my hair, making it fall to my shoulders, then delicately placed the orange hairband atop my head.

'You look so gorgeous,' she said, a little teary-eyed.

'Oh, don't get all emotional on me, Lu. I am so sorry I didn't tell you. It was because I thought maybe you liked Sunil and would be jealous of me going on a date with him. Please, forgive me.'

Lu said nothing, just hugged me and cried. Even I was confused now. Were they tears of joy because I came clean with the story or of sadness because she was indeed in love with Sunil?

After about thirty seconds of hugging, she pushed me away and said, 'You deserve to find love and happiness, something I will never know again.'

She kissed me on the cheek and rushed me to finish getting ready, so I would not be late. The memories of what Lu went through with Angelo came into my head, and I felt deeply sorry for her. For a moment, I wished it was her in my place, going on a date and discovering love. She deserved it, probably more than me. So, I promised myself I would make the most out of it and show Lu that there was still goodness and love in the world, maybe inspiring her to give romance another chance.

When I walked downstairs at three o'clock, Sunil was already waiting. He first looked at me and immediately turned his head away, as if he had seen someone he was avoiding. A few seconds later, he looked again, frowned, forcefully blinked a few times, and then smiled. He looked handsome, with gel in his hair, and he was wearing a green short-sleeved shirt which made him look bigger than he was.

'Good afternoon, Lady Aubrey,' he whispered with an insinuating smile. Sunil had a gentle way of making a woman feel special. Much different from his friend Marvan, who indeed was better looking, but as I'd figured out, had no manners or respect for women.

'You look even more beautiful today,' he praised me. 'Is this a new dress?'

I was going to lie and say yes, but the earlier event with Lu was still fresh in my mind and lying did not sit well with me at that moment.

'No, not really. My friend Lu loaned it to me. But thanks for the compliment.'

His face went blank when I said Lu's name, but I did not want to read too much into his reactions. He quickly held my hand and rushed us to the bus stop, so we would not miss the bus to Za'abeel Park.

The ride to the park took less time than I thought. Sunil kept looking at the picnic bag I brought along with all sorts of delicacies, but I made sure he did not have a chance to taste any of the goodies until we arrived.

Za'abeel Park was an oasis in the middle of Dubai. Escaping the dust and ugly architecture of the compound we lived in and going to a green area, full of tall trees with a lake in the middle, was absolutely amazing. The place was full of families having barbecues, children playing on the grass, and a cricket match going on. How funny that the celebration of independence from the British involved people playing a typical British game. For some reason, everybody at the park looked Indian to me. Sunil was excited about watching the game but made a special effort to find a quiet area where we could place our mat on the grass, sit down, and chat, while nibbling on my favourite merienda recipes: *bibingkang* (cassava cake), *palitaw* (sweet rice dumplings), *puto* (muffins with cheese), and *biko* (sticky rice cake with caramel).

Sunil seemed to appreciate the food and was forever complimenting me, mentioning my cooking skills and the way I looked. It became hard to move away from him every time he tried to touch my hair, saying it smelled good, or play with the end of my dress, which lay on top of the mat we were sitting on.

We sat at the edge of the park, next to a metal fence which separated the park from the outside path. Just across from us, maybe ten meters away, we saw an Indian family sitting on the grass outside the park. Although there were only six family members, they managed to unload enough paraphernalia from the car to cater to an entire village. They set up a blue camping tent and the two children ran inside it to play. With not much going on outside the park, the family looked at us as part of their entertainment. Our privacy had been broken.

Sunil suggested we move to another spot, perhaps more private, but I was afraid he would try a more direct approach, which could put both of us in prison for public indecency.

'I don't think anywhere else in the park will be emptier,' I said.

'I will go have a look around anyway,' he answered.

'Wait. There is no point. When we came in, the park was already full. You saw how many people had arrived since we got here. It is best if we just stay and talk. Let's just enjoy the day. Besides, there are no children right next to us, screaming or crying.'

He nodded and sat down, very much against his will. He knew I was right.

We spent a lovely afternoon, holding hands and sharing details about our past. Sunil said he never had a girlfriend before and this was all very new to him. After a couple of hours, we gathered our things and crossed the bridge which connected both sides of the park, divided by a highway. The other side was just as full, but it had the benefit of being closer to the area where the fireworks would happen.

At eight o'clock sharp, we watched the most beautiful fireworks spectacle right above our heads. Sunil sat on the grass and let me put my head on his lap, so I could see the lights illuminating the sky without getting a neckache. The show lasted almost ten minutes and when it finished, I continued lying down, with Sunil looking at my face and stroking my hair all the way from the roots to the very tips. He held the orange satin headband in his left hand and told me he preferred me with my hair down, and nothing holding it back. He shoved the headband in the bag with the food containers and made a tight knot on the top, as if it were alive and would try to escape.

I started to worry about the time and Sunil read my mind.

'We should get going,' he said. 'It will take a while until we get home.'

He lifted my shoulders up and as I was preparing to stand, he placed one of his hands under my dress and slid it across my thigh. I froze, my cheeks burning and my face turning red. An electric shock came down my spine, at the same time paralysing me and activating the animal instinct in my body. I stood there, completely immobilised, for what felt like an eternity, although I knew it was just a couple of seconds.

Sunil stood up, leaned over, and whispered in my ear, 'We really should go somewhere more private.'

I was excited but unsure if this was what I really wanted. We had not even kissed yet and I felt it was all moving too fast. At first, he claimed that he was inexperienced with girls and that he never had a girlfriend and now he was acting very audaciously.

He grabbed the bag and helped me stand up, patting the back of his trousers to get rid of the grass. We walked in silence to the bus stop, and when the bus came, he insisted on getting in first and choosing the seat. He picked one at the very end of the bus, holding my hand and dragging me with him. He let me sit by the window, claiming I would appreciate the view of the city as we headed home. The traffic had increased significantly, and we knew it would take us around an hour and a half to get home.

I felt better that we were already on our way. Luckily, we lived in the same building, so it was a direct route for both of us and he would see me through the front door. Maricar often warned us to be careful at night in that neighbourhood and I felt safe with Sunil. At least until he started sliding his fingers alongside my skirt, touching the outside of my thigh with his right hand. I blushed again and moved my leg away from his hand. He insisted and, reaching the bottom of my skirt, he slid his hand underneath it and between my legs, holding my inner thigh and moving his hand up and down. I desperately tried to stop him, afraid someone would see. The bus had cameras installed and the punishment for public exposure ranged from deportation to long jail sentences.

Who *was* this guy, anyway? Why was he so different from the Sunil I thought I knew? What had happened?

I tried to grab the top part of his arm and push it away, but he squeezed my left thigh, hurting me. Then he brought his face close to mine and said, 'Don't you dare move! If you say anything, scream, or move, I will claim you were harassing me on the bus and ask for the police. Do you know what they do to prostitutes in this country?'

His face was serious, almost angry. I did not recognise the man beside me. How could I have been so foolish and believed he would be different from his best friend, Marvan?

For the next forty minutes, Sunil played with my body, his hand covered by the loose skirt of my dress. The thigh-to-knee movement became thigh-to-crotch movement and he freely touched my underwear until he managed to find a way inside it. I turned my face against the window, so nobody would see my tears as he lowered my panties down my legs. What had been pure discomfort was now becoming pain, and Sunil made no attempt to stop.

The bus got emptier with each stop and, for the last fifteen minutes of the ride, there was just us and another man sitting at the front of the bus. Sunil placed the bag with the empty food containers on my lap and, pretending to be looking into the bag, he pulled the top of my dress away and slid one of his hands inside it, touching my breasts.

I tried to stop him again, fruitlessly. He grabbed my hand and placed it on his lap, telling me to get to work. I did not know what he meant. I'd never had a sexual encounter before. All my knowledge was based on stories from the other girls, but I had never touched a man before. I wondered if I squeezed his private parts hard enough, he would let me go, but given that he lived in the same building, I felt I would not be able to run away fast enough to escape him.

Sunil saw my shock and lack of movement and placed his hand on top of mine, massaging himself over his trousers.

When we arrived at our stop, I felt relief. Sunil stood up, told me to put myself together, and held my hand tightly so I would not run away. We exited the bus and he placed his arm around my shoulders, holding me close to him. I was crying again, continuous tears rolling down my cheeks, scared of what this man was going to do to me.

'Why are you doing this, Sunil?'

'Don't pretend to be naïve, Aubrey. I know you Filipinas are all sluts.'

'How can you say that? After all the time we spent together?'

'To be quite honest, I would have preferred to spend time alone with Lu than having you hanging around with us all the time.'

'What... how can you... how can you say that?'

'Listen Aubrey. Enough with the pretending. I tried to get Lu to go out with me so many times I've lost count. I am sure you were aware of it, weren't you? After all, aren't you best friends?'

I was sure we were, and this could only mean that Sunil was lying.

'Every time I received a *no* as an answer,' he continued, 'she would turn up the next day all charming and flirtatious. I kept insisting, but all that bitch could say was, *I can't!* So, after all my requests were denied, my advances were made fun of, and my gifts were rejected, I decided to move on to the next available girl: You.'

'What? You really fancied Lu, not me?'

'Hahaha. You are a good actress!'

Once again, I was speechless, my head aching with too much information and deceit.

'And the trick with the headband?' he said, his voice getting angrier.

'What?'

'I gave this headband to Lu as a present last week, in my last attempt to get her pretty body into my bed. But no! She ditched me coldly, saying there was no room for men in her life. Who did she think she was? She is very beautiful, clearly, but let me tell you: She is not Miss Universe! She is a maid who cleans toilets around town!'

He paused, his face as red as an active volcano. His right hand was squeezing my forearm so hard I thought he would break my bones.

'And she kept the hairband,' he continued. 'So, when you showed up wearing it, I knew you would play hard-to-get also.'

He paused, looking at me as I sobbed uncontrollably.

'You know,' he said with a smirk, 'this might become an interesting game after all!'

I was disgusted. The man I fell in love with was a pervert, a rapist. I was considered the back-up plan and now he wanted to sadistically turn this into a game. How much worse could it get?

I tried to move away from him again, but he held me tight. Sunil was skinny but strong and made no attempt to let me go.

'Stop trying to get away,' he ordered me, his voice upset. 'We are going into the building and straight to my accommodation. Marvan is out and I have the room all to myself. We will have an incredible night... I will make you see fireworks all night long.'

My body became rigid, frightened, knowing rape was next on his list. We turned the corner and arrived at our street. I started to walk faster and faster, knowing there were only a few more buildings until we reached the entrance of our apartment block. I hoped that there would be people standing outside, to whom I could cry for help. Anyone who looked at me would see the amount of distress I was in, and hopefully would stop to at least ask what was going on, which would give me the opportunity to run upstairs and lock myself in the house.

To my disappointment, the street was empty, not a single soul in sight. The lights in the apartments were off and I wondered if everyone was sleeping or out partying. Sunil gave me the bag to hold, opened the front door with his right hand, and kept his free hand holding tightly to mine so I would not escape. We moved upstairs, and I knew we would have to pass in front of my accommodation's door before reaching his.

The corridor was dark and silent. Sunil walked fast, dragging me behind him. At the end of the hall, I could see my apartment door was closed. Sunil smiled, knowing we were just a few steps away from his sexual encounter. When we were exactly in front of my apartment door, it opened abruptly. Lu stepped outside.

'Aubrey, are you okay?' she asked.

I could not answer, tears rolling down my cheeks.

Lu realised the severity of the situation and, being the brave woman that she was, she brought her right arm from behind her back, revealing a large kitchen knife.

'Sunil, you bastard!' she shouted. 'Let her go right now!'

Lu advanced into the corridor, placing the knife closer to Sunil's face.

Sunil let go of my hand, and I took this one moment of freedom to run inside the house and lock myself in the bathroom. I did not hear any more voices, just the slamming of the front door and angry steps in the living room coming towards the bathroom. I assumed it was Lu, although she said nothing. The person stood outside the bathroom door for about five minutes, I guess hoping for me to come out, but I was too upset and confused about what to do next. I turned the shower on and stepped inside, fully dressed. The shower area had light-green tiles on the walls and floor and was surrounded by a plastic curtain which made the water sound like rain when it fell against it. I did not care about ruining Lu's dress. I just sat on the floor and cried like I had never cried before. The rain-like sound was soothing. The hot water running down my neck and back washed away the ugliness of the situation I had put myself in. Between my legs, I saw the water running towards the drain turn red, and then clear again, washing away the blood in my underwear.

I stayed there for at least forty-five minutes, long enough for me to get in trouble with the other women, as the water and electricity bills would be astronomical. Electricity was expensive in general, but water was a luxury item, prices running sky-high due to the cost of desalination plants in a desert country. Still, I stayed there a little longer. No thoughts came to my mind at all. It was as if a black cloud had invaded my mind and there was only the feeling of the water running down my body; the peaceful rain rolling on the plastic curtain.

I had been under the shower for quite a while when Maricar knocked on the door.

'Are you okay in there, Aubrey?'

I was still crying and could not muster any words to answer her. I just turned off the shower, took my wet clothes off, and wrapped myself in a towel. Maricar knocked again.

'Sweetie, let me in. We can talk.'

I opened the door, just a little, enough to see if she was alone. I opened the door a little more and Maricar slid inside the bathroom, locking the door behind her.

'We are all worried about you. What happened, my dear?'

'I... I've been a fool...' And I started to sob again, hugging Maricar in such desperation that she became even more worried.

'Are you hurt? Do you need to go to the hospital? Talk to me, Aubrey!'

It took me almost an hour to explain to Maricar all that had happened. I would stop every now and then to blow my nose and wipe the tears off my face. Maricar was gentle and motherly and did not rush me or pressure me to disclose anything I was not comfortable with. I told her the entire story, and to my surprise, Maricar told me that Lu was sitting in the living room, crying uncontrollably, telling everyone she had ruined my life. Maricar asked me if it was okay for her to let me be alone for just a few minutes, so she could tell Lu that I would be all right.

I consented with a nod but did not think I would ever be all right again in my life.

As Maricar left me, I relived the events again and again in my mind, thinking, *what could I have done?* I stopped feeling sorry for myself and started getting upset for being so naïve and blind. How could I have not seen this? Why did I have to wait for Lu to come and rescue me? Why didn't I just kick Sunil in the balls and run away?

A while later, Maricar knocked on the door, came in, and told me how deeply sorry Lu was. She begged me to speak to her and offered to be by my side the whole time if I wanted to. Despite my miserable lack of luck, I felt blessed to have Maricar as a comforting shoulder to cry on. I accepted her plea and her offer to grab my pyjamas from my locker, so I could change and go straight to the bedroom without having to explain myself to the other women in the accommodation. She came back a minute or so later with my pyjamas and my toothbrush. I took the dress off and as I was drying myself, I noticed the bruises on my inner thighs and on my forearm. The physical pain was intense, but the emotional pain was unbearable.

I walked to my bedroom and found Lu sitting on the bottom bunk of one of the bunkbeds, alone, in the dark. Certainly, all the other women were in the living room, gossiping about my disgrace, but I did not care. I walked in, closed the door and stood there in silence for a while.

'Would you like to sit next to me, so we can talk?' asked Lu.

Even though the lights were off, I could see Lu's silhouette in the dim light coming from under the door. I moved towards her and sat down a foot away from her, on the hard mattress. With no warning, she jumped on top of me, embracing me tightly and kissing my forehead.

'I am so sorry!' she said, sobbing. 'I should have told you to stay away from Sunil. I should have told you to stay away from *all* men. They are all the same. I can't believe Sunil actually hurt you. I am so sorry... so sorry.'

I reluctantly hugged her back, and we sat in silence again, digesting what had happened. When we spoke again, the first thing Lu said was, 'Please forgive me.' She felt guilty for having rejected Sunil and thought it was her fault that he sought revenge by raping me. She was consumed with remorse for having given me the hairband and claimed she should have told me about Sunil's flirtatious approaches towards her.

I wasn't sure what to feel towards her. Lu was my best friend but in all my pain, I felt deceived. I wished she had confided in me, and told me about Sunil's intentions. This was the second time she'd hid something from me. The first time, involving Angelo, I understood it was a police order and she could not disclose anything. But now, there was no reason for her to have kept it from me.

Lu cried some more and hugged me again. She held my hands tightly and I felt her sweaty palms as she explained that, ultimately, she wanted to believe that people could change, that Sunil could be a good guy and that I could fall in love and be happy.

That was pleasant to hear and made sense in my brain. But my heart was broken; I felt used, cheated.

'Something inside of me felt strange after you left for the date,' she said with a soft voice. 'Call it a sixth sense. I don't know. But I kept looking through the windows all night, waiting for you to return so I could check on you.'

'Yes, you just saved my life,' I told her, acknowledging the obvious fact but also resentful that she'd put me in this situation in the first place. 'If it wasn't for you holding that knife, my fate would have been much, much worse,' I continued with a pinch of sarcasm.

'No, please Aubrey. It is not like that. I was stupid to begin with. I made so many mistakes. Please forgive me.' Her eyes filled with tears again.

It broke my heart seeing Lu like that. She had always been the independent, fearless woman who once told me we should all be brave and stand up for ourselves. Maybe it was my fault that all of this happened. Maybe it was nobody's fault. Maybe it was destined to happen to teach us all a lesson. Nevertheless, it was now in my power to decide if she should carry the burden of guilt forever or live a life with a friend to count on. How could I possibly decide someone's fate if I was not in control of my own destiny?

Something very strange happened at that moment. As if struck by lightning, my entire body became filled with energy. It was like I was high on drugs. I could feel sparkles brightening up my eyes and warmth filling my soul.

'Of course, I forgive you, Lu,' I said, hugging her again. 'What happened to me tonight was not your fault at all. Sunil is a horrible person… he is the one who deserves to burn in hell or go to jail or both!' I vented, wiping my tears away.

My heart was beating fast and I felt empowered, strong, and for the first time, I realised I was no longer a girl but a woman. I was still disappointed at Lu for not telling me the truth but forgiving her felt good. I was confident that time would mend out relationship.

It was getting very late and Maricar reminded us that we would be waking up early the next day, and the other women needed to go bed soon. She suggested we go to the police station the next day and report Sunil, but I was not so certain about the idea.

'He will lie,' I said. 'It will be my word against his.'

'We can see the bruises on your body, Aubrey. This is enough evidence,' Maricar reassured me.

'That is probably the best revenge you can get,' said Lu. 'We will go with you after work tomorrow.' Marciar nodded in agreement.

I gave Lu one last hug, and when we broke apart and she walked away, I felt the pain coming back at full power. The strength I had felt a moment ago vanished. A dark cloud engulfed my thoughts, the bravery of my forgiveness was gone, and I started to cry again, continuing to cry all through the night, until my body felt so exhausted that it gave in and I slept, wishing I had died instead.

# 13

# ACCIDENTS HAPPEN

The next morning, the alarm rang as usual and before I opened my eyes, I wished the previous night had only been a dream. Unfortunately, it hadn't, and it took less than five minutes for everybody to pounce on me, asking me questions about what had happened. I hid under the sheets, closed my eyes, and again wished I was dead. The pain, both physical and emotional, was unbearable and the questioning did not make things easier. How I wished I could just disappear, vanish from this planet. Maybe I would get lucky and get struck by lightning today. Death sounded like a promising idea indeed.

Maricar walked into my room, elbowing people away and telling them to mind their own businesses. I got dressed and skipped breakfast, as I was feeling nauseated and at this stage, I would do anything to avoid having to interact with anyone who wanted to ask me more questions. I waited for Maricar by the door and we walked down the stairs together.

I had told Maricar I did not feel safe being in the building, not knowing when Sunil would attack me again. She promised to be by my side at all times and reassured me by putting a small pocket knife inside my purse.

'Just take it out and stab the son of a bitch!' she said, grinning.

That was the first and only time I heard Maricar swear. She kept her word and did not leave my side until the van arrived. I quickly opened the front passenger door and sat next to Rizalino, who looked puzzled by my presence in the front seat but asked no questions. He merely tapped his seatbelt twice in a gesture to show that I should fasten mine.

At work, I got assigned a villa in the Umm Sequim area, a residential part of town with large villas, often with ample gardens and swimming pools. I would spend the entire day working in one of these and because of the size of the mansion, two people would be allocated to the job. How unlucky I was! That was all I dreaded, to have to work alongside someone else asking me questions as we went along. Fortunately, I had a friend looking after me. The moment it was announced that Honorata would be joining me, Maricar grabbed her arm, looked into her eyes, and said something which made Honorata lower her head and nod. Despite all the disgrace that had happened to me the evening before, I felt lucky to have Maricar to watch my back.

The client's villa was, as expected, large and sumptuous, and stood less than a block from the beach.

'Come in, come in,' said the tall brunette woman, waving her hands in the air. 'You.' She pointed at Honorata.

'Go inside and I will tell you what to do in a second. And you.' She pointed at me, her nicely manicured nails shining with bright red nail polish. 'Start by cleaning the front gate and then the area around the swimming pool. I want the front gate scrubbed with sanitizer so the smell of urine from the pigs who visited my front door yesterday is removed completely. Then you should clean the fence surrounding the swimming pool, the lamps, and the stone floor.'

The brunette turned around and started to walk quickly towards the front door of the house.

'Helen! Helen!' she shouted, almost hysterically.

A young black woman came outside and took instructions from her Madam. Immediately after, she walked towards me and introduced herself as Helen, the ex-housemaid, recently promoted to nanny. She was proud of her new job title and I wondered if that came with a pay raise, but I could not bother to ask. I was told to start the cleaning by the main gate.

On a shitty day, there was nothing more fitting than cleaning urine from the street. I did not ask how it happened, but Helen volunteered an explanation while handing me the cleaning products I would need for the day's job.

'It happens almost every weekend,' she started. 'People come to the beach, park their cars somewhere around here, sometimes even blocking the front gate. This is a popular part of the beach, free of charge and easily accessible. They come in masses, especially the young men, sometimes six or seven packed inside one car. With no public bathrooms around, they relieve themselves along the villa's walls, in particular at this stretch of dusty road leading to the beach.' And she pointed at the brown wall, about two meters tall, which surrounded the villa.

'Do you want me to clean the entire wall?' I asked, expressionless.

'No, no. Just the front gate. Scrub it well with the yellow disinfectant and then rinse with plenty of water.'

I nodded and wondered where I should fetch water to rinse the gate, but I did not bother to ask. I could always just fill the bucket with the swimming pool water.

The gate scrubbing took longer than I expected and the smell coming from it was repulsive. I felt good cleaning it, almost as penitence for my awful day yesterday. From the outside of the villa, I could see the ocean at the end of the street, the blue water inviting me for a swim. How I wished I could have run over there, swam to the deepest parts of it, and drowned inconspicuously.

I sighed, picked up the bucket, and went inside to clean the pool. It stood at the corner of the garden, square-shaped and quite big. The fence around it was made of a contorted metal which accumulated dust in every single turn and bend. I assumed it was there to avoid accidents, like children falling into it. A strong water-pressure gun would have done the job in five minutes but instead, I was given a brush slightly bigger than a toothbrush and a bucket of water. I scrubbed and scrubbed, and tears rolled down my face once again.

'Hey, you!' Madam's voice called from a distance. 'Make sure you replace the lightbulbs on the lampposts around the pool, too. I have switched the power off, so there is no risk of you getting electrocuted. Just grab a few of these,' she said, holding a lightbulb above her head, 'and insert them in the empty sockets.' She placed the lightbulb package on the floor and closed the door behind her.

I immediately dropped the brush and went to fetch the package left by the door. There were ten units in the pack and I started to count the lamps. There were five lampposts surrounding the pool, placed about one meter from the edge of the water. Each lamppost had three sockets, symmetrically distributed at the top. The posts were not very tall, and the hanging sockets were just the right height for me to be able to insert the lightbulbs without using a ladder. There were eight lightbulbs missing in total. I assumed the ones in place were good and functional, and I decided I would not bother to check if they weren't.

The fence cleaning job was so tedious that I decided to replace the pool bulbs immediately. I flipped the water bucket over and placed the pack of lightbulbs on top of it because the floor around the swimming pool was completely wet from the fence washing. I replaced two in the first lamppost, then two more in the second and one in the third. The fourth lamppost had no bulbs at all and I held two bulbs with one hand and a third with the other hand. This was the lamppost which stood closer to the edge of the swimming pool and the floor around it had puddles touching its base. I worried for a moment but remembered Madam saying she had switched the main power off. I put the first bulb in but let it slip out of my hand as I turned to screw it in. It fell on the floor and broke into a million tiny pieces of glass.

'Damn,' I thought to myself, as I realised I would have to clean it.

I looked around, hoping nobody saw it and went on to screw in the other two bulbs already in my hands. As I put the next one in, I felt a tingling sensation in my fingers and then everything turned black.

What a wonderful feeling! For a moment, the pain in my soul went away. The weight of the world was taken from my shoulders. The memories of the day before disappeared. Lightness. A truly peaceful sense of nothing.

# 14

# HOSPITAL

'Aubrey. Aubrey, can you hear me?' A male voice asked.

*Oh, heavens!* I thought. *This is what the afterlife is like! How relaxing and calm.*

I wondered if the voice calling me belonged to an angel or God Himself. Maybe I was being too presumptuous by thinking I went straight to heaven, but surely hell would not feel so good. I saw a light in the distance and tried to focus my eyes on it.

'Aubrey, can you hear me?' the voice asked again, this time a bit louder.

I still could not see anything, just the bright light getting bigger and bigger, closer to me. My body felt warm and weightless. I tried to move my head to the side to see the angel calling me, but I could not move.

'Aubrey, can you hear me?' the voice insisted.

'Are you sure she will wake up?' a familiar female voice whispered.

'Shush. Give her time,' the male voice said again. 'Aubrey, this is Doctor Sayeed. Can you hear me? If you can, just squeeze my hand,' he said in a calm voice.

The bright light was now shining on my face, so close I could almost touch it. My body went from feeling warmth to heat and then *intense* heat, all in a matter of seconds. Something was not right and, no matter how much I tried to move my body, it did not respond. Suddenly, the darkness approached me again and all thoughts were gone from my head.

When I opened my eyes for the first time after inserting that lightbulb in its socket, I found myself in a hospital bed with soft white bed linens covering me and baby blue walls all around. There were two more patients in the room with me, both laying in beds on my left side. On my right, there was a window and it looked like a bright, sunny day outside. The patients next to me were either sleeping or dead, as neither of them moved at all. I know this because I stared at them for what seemed like an eternity. All I heard was the sound of my own heart through the monitor, beeping away in the quietness of the room. My mouth was dry but there was no water in sight. I pulled the top sheet off, so I could try to get out of bed and as I looked down to my legs, I saw them covered in bandages all the way from my ankles to the tops of my thighs. I also had a bandage on my stomach, which had a splash of blood on it and a very large piece of gauze with a covering net all the way up my right arm. I freaked out and the heart monitor began to beep incessantly, alerting the nurses in the corridor.

Two of them came into the room hurriedly and they looked happy to see me.

'Stay down, Aubrey,' said the first nurse, holding my shoulder and repositioning me in the bed. One of my legs had fallen off the bed and was squeezing the urine bag hanging off the metal hook attached to the bedframe. The nurse lifted my leg into place and muttered gentle, calming words to me.

Meanwhile, the second nurse pushed a red button on the top of the bed and went outside, telling the other nurse she was going to fetch Doctor Sayeed on the third floor.

About ten minutes later, a tall, Arab-looking man wearing grey trousers and a white overcoat entered the room, accompanied by the second nurse. He also smiled when he saw me and with both hands clasped together, he said loudly, *'Mashallah!* A miracle! *Mashallah!'*

Two other nurses entered the room and I realised I had a captive audience. I was confused and had many questions for them. Where to start? How did I get here? Why was I a miracle? What was with all the bandages? However, I was exhausted and the effort it would take to open my mouth seemed gigantic at that time. I closed my eyes just to blink, but found it took me about a minute to reopen them. I must have been given drugs or something because when the doctor spoke, his voice was in slow motion, each syllable pausing before entering my ears.

'I am Doctor Sayeed,' he said. 'I am in charge of looking after you here at the hospital. Do you know where you are?' he asked, smiling.

I shook my head negatively and my neck felt funny, sore, and stiff.

'You were brought to this hospital after you suffered an electrocution.' He paused, wondering if I understood what he had said. 'An electric shock.' He paused again. I guess I did not move, because he stopped his explanation, and looking into my eyes, he whispered, 'I am glad you are alive. You were in a coma for almost two weeks and it is natural that you may be feeling a little disoriented and tired. Just take your time. Rest and we will talk again this afternoon.' He left the room and I immediately fell asleep, ignoring the presence of the nurses around me.

I do not know how long I slept, but when I opened my eyes again, it was dark outside.

'Thank God you are awake, Aubrey,' said Mariann with her hand up in the air, praising the Lord.

'Hello, my dear,' said Maricar, gently holding my hand. She stroked my hair and her eyes filled up with tears.

'Oh, stop it, you sissy woman!' reprimanded Mariann, punching Maricar in the shoulder. The punch must have hurt because Maricar turned around, and looking into Mariann's eyes, she said in a deep, upset voice, 'You either behave or get out. Aubrey does not need your attitude right now.

'How are you feeling?' asked Maricar, turning her attention to me.

'I am a bit dizzy. What happened to me?'

'Honorata found you passed out by the side of the swimming pool in the house you two were cleaning. You were laying down on the wet stone floor, with a few cuts on your legs, a large cut on your belly, and the skin on your arms and hands burned. They told us you got electrocuted while changing a lightbulb and it burned your extremities. You must have fallen down on the top of the lightbulbs because pieces of glass cut your legs and a large piece perforated your abdomen.'

She paused, her eyes full of tears. She opened her mouth to speak but no sound came out. She took a tissue from her pocket, blew her nose, and tried again. 'You lost a lot of blood, my dear. At one stage, the doctors didn't think you would make it.' She started to cry loudly, and I finally comprehended the seriousness of the situation.

'You will be okay now,'' she said while wiping away her tears.

'My stomach hurts,' I said. 'Can I have some water?'

'Here, my dear.' Maricar handed me a plastic cup.

I only took a couple of sips and immediately felt nauseated.

'Take it easy. You had fifteen stitches in your belly. They were removed already but your muscles are weak, and it will take some time for you to recover.'

'What is wrong with my arms?' I asked, looking at the bandages.

'They got burned from the shock,' answered a nurse who had just entered the room. 'We had to scrape off some of the skin and flesh, but you are lucky we didn't have to amputate your hands. Don't rub the bandages and the recovery will be swift. Hopefully, you will barely notice the scars after a few months.'

'Is that how long will it take for me to recover?'

'In two weeks, all the bandages will come off and in one month, it should be properly healed. Don't worry, you will be fine.' I closed my eyes to avoid the tears welling up and as my eyelids got heavier, I fell asleep again, enjoying the sedatives in my bloodstream.

A week later, Wasim came to see me in hospital.

'Aubrey, what happened to you was awful," he started to say, standing by my bed, pretending to be concerned about my health. 'How are you feeling?'

I was about to answer him when he pulled out a chair and changed the look on his face to a more severe, business-oriented one.

'We need to discuss what we are going to do with you. You will be discharged from the hospital soon and I will arrange for you to go back to the Philippines and be with your family.'

'But I don't...' I started to say but I was unable to finish the sentence because he interrupted me once again.

'Don't you worry, your plane ticket will be paid for and these days you spent in hospital will be added to your salary.' He was smiling a victorious grin. 'Go to sleep, and I will arrange everything. Is there anyone you want me to contact on your behalf?' He paused for a second and stood up, tapping my hand exactly where the IV was inserted, which hurt a lot, and then left the room without bothering to get the name of my relatives or their phone numbers.

Seven days later, Doctor Sayeed came for his routine visit and announced that I would be discharged in four days. He asked how I was doing and if he could do anything else to help me. Doctor Sayeed had a smooth voice and something about him inspired trust. I felt this was my opportunity to reach out to the only person who could truly help me: Danda. I was fed up with having the people who worked and lived with me coming for visits in the evenings, and I knew Wasim was going to get rid of me as soon as I was discharged. This could not be the end of my journey... I had to do something.

Going home was not an option, not after all I had been through.

'Can I stay longer, Doctor Sayeed?'

'You are recovering well and will be fine at home. Do you have any family here?'

I shook my head. 'Only a friend from home. Her name is Danda, can you please call her for me? Ask her to come see me as soon as possible?'

'Sure. Just give me her number and I will be in touch with her. You need to rest. A *lot* of rest. No work for at least another two weeks and you should avoid getting your arms and hands wet.'

'I have no help at the compound, Doctor Sayeed. Please keep me in the hospital for at least another week so I can organise my life,' I said desperately, panic taking over my voice and my eyes filling up with tears. 'My friend Danda will help, but I need you to keep me here a little longer.' Tears were now rolling down my cheeks. 'Please.'

The next day, Danda came to see me after work.

'Oh my God, Aubrey! I could not believe it when the hospital called me! Are you okay? What happened to you?'

'I am fine now, Danda. I am so happy you are here! I did not know who else to contact.' My hands were shaking, and my heart exploded with all the emotions I had been hiding over the last few days. Tears rolled down my cheeks like a waterfall and my nose got blocked from all the sobbing. After about fifteen minutes of sitting there, just hugging each other, I got my breath back and explained to her what had happened to me as she listened attentively, never interrupting me, and then asked several questions that nobody else had ever asked me before.

'What is the nationality of the clients you were working for?'

'English, I think,' I answered with a puzzled expression.

'Did your work make you sign any documents?'

'Wasim came by two days ago with some papers, which he said were standard documents needed to settle the hospital charges. I didn't read them properly. But I also didn't sign anything because Doctor Sayeed told me not to rush anything while I was still on painkillers.'

'That is good. Aubrey. Have the clients been in contact with you? Did they visit you in hospital?'

I shook my head negatively.

'Do you have health insurance from work?'

I shook my head again.

Danda smiled a fake smile and said, 'Leave it to me, sweetie. Don't worry. Just make sure you do not sign anything, and I will be back to see you in a few days. Do not leave the hospital until I get here, okay?'

'Okay.'

'Promise me!'

'I promise, Danda.'

She left, looking worried, and I stood there, looking at the mute TV, on which a cookery programme was playing with no sound.

## 15

# INSURANCE AND ASSURANCE

It was a beautiful morning outside. The cleaners had cleaned the windows outside my room and I could see the cloudless blue sky outside. Two days had passed since Danda came to visit me and I knew Doctor Sayeed would come in any minute to conclude my discharge from the hospital. Where would I go? How would I pay the hospital bills? Would Wasim send me back to the Philippines? Could I take some painkillers home?

The pain in my arms and hands was bearable but the cut on my belly still hurt every time I moved from side to side. At around twelve o'clock, Danda rushed into the room, smiling and speaking rapidly with excitement.

'Hello, hello! How are you today? Feeling better? I have great news …'

She was so ecstatic and speaking so frantically that I had no chance to answer her initial questions.

'...I found out that your employer has been charging the villa client for all your expenses! Everything. Ambulance, hospital, surgeries, and now they are asking for loss of working days and emotional and physical damages! I don't assume Wasim mentioned any of this to you, did he?'

'No,' I answered in shock. 'How did you find out?'

'I went to the villa where your accident happened and spoke to the English family. At first, when I introduced myself, they told me to go away and said they were fed up with the blackmailing and that I should go and hire a lawyer, but then I told them I was your cousin and I was afraid for your life. The lady let me in and explained that your employer had sent a man called Wasim there the day after your accident, who at first demanded money for bills and later started to threaten them with a lawsuit for negligence and unplanned manslaughter.'

'What is negligence? And mans-what?'

'Don't worry about that. The important thing is that she was scared and upset by his demands. When I knocked on her door, she thought I also worked for that company. It was just after I explained I didn't that she opened up. She asked me to come back the following day when her husband would be home.'

'And did you go back?'

'Yes, of course. When I got there the next evening, she opened the door and welcomed me in. Her husband was in the living room talking to another man. Both men were wearing dark suits and speaking quickly in English. Her husband, Michael Baker, was a tall man, with dark hair going grey at the sides and thick-framed glasses that made him look more Italian than English. The other man was short and slightly bald, Pakistani-looking. Mr Baker introduced him only as his lawyer. He told me to sit down and started to ask me questions about the company you worked for, about you and so on. We spoke for almost four hours. In the end, they asked me to leave the room and go to the kitchen. Their house helper didn't look pleased to see me, and only offered me a glass of water because her Madam came in and asked her where her manners had been.

'The private meeting went on for at least forty-five minutes and I was getting nervous. Maybe they were plotting something that would be bad for you. Maybe to get you arrested for incompetence... I don't know. My mind was racing, and I realised nobody knew I was there. They called me into the living room again and this time, asked me to sit between the two men on the large sofa.

'I sat down, and nobody spoke. They just looked at each other as if communicating with their eyes, saying: *Who will break the news to this poor woman?*

'The lawyer was the one who spoke first. He told me they were being blackmailed by your employer and that they were going to go to the police and report them. But they needed your help and were willing to make a deal with you.'

My face became paralysed. What did Danda mean by 'a deal'? And the police were now involved! My worst fears were coming true. I questioned my judgement in asking Danda for her help. Maybe it would have been best if I had just shut my mouth, signed the papers Wasim gave me to sign, and pretended nothing had happened. I suspect Danda saw the fear in my face as she sat on the bed close to me and gave me a hug.

As if rehearsed and part of a play, the heart monitor of the patient next to me started to beep incessantly. Nurses rushed in to check her vital signs. The patient's heart rate calmed down and she was able to explain that she just got a bit emotional over something she remembered. When the nurses left the room, she turned to Danda and me and said in a confident, dictatorial voice, 'You better thank your friend, girl. And take the fucking deal, whatever it is. A mean Pakistani boss or an Englishman with a lawyer? Hm...' And she made a face, indicating that I was being stupid for not seeing the obvious.

'Go on, Danda,' I said, trying to ignore this stranger's piece of advice.

Danda explained that the Bakers would pay for all my hospital expenses and would offer me a job in their house, with a one-year contract to be a nanny to their three-month-old baby girl. They would take care of my visa, give me an accommodation, and anything else possible so I wouldn't have to go back to that cleaning firm or back to the Philippines. When she said that, my heart lifted, and I thought I would faint. She went on and told me that she had negotiated a salary for me which was more than double what I was making before and that the Baker family had agreed to only start the position once I was fully recovered, especially from my deeper wounds.

But they also wanted something in return. I would have to refuse to go back to my accommodation after my discharge from the hospital, I would have to go to the police and explain my version of the accident, which was officially registered wrongly by Wasim, and most importantly, I would have to take the documents Wasim wanted me to sign from him, without signing them and without telling him. These documents would be entered as evidence to support the case.

I agreed immediately to the terms but explained to Danda that the discharge date was today and Doctor Sayeed and Wasim could enter through the door at any time, telling me to go. Danda hugged me again and told me not to worry. She had taken the day off and told me the Bakers were paying her a fee for her help. I felt happy for Danda, feeling less guilty for having bothered her with my own problems. She kissed me twice on the cheeks and said she would go and wait downstairs in the hospital cafeteria. She would stay there for as long as necessary, until I got discharged. She thought Wasim would come to pick me up and told me that I should try to get the documents then. I should then refuse to go with him and come find her in the cafeteria, where she would call the Bakers and they would come get us.

Fear took over my body as Danda stood up to leave, and the only thing stopping me from crying was the lady in the bed next to mine, her eyes wide open and her grin showing her approval and satisfaction.

At around two o'clock, Doctor Sayeed came to see me and broke the already expected news.

'Good afternoon, Aubrey,' he said, smiling.

I smiled back, wondering if he knew something I didn't.

'I think you are ready to go home, my dear. I was told your boss will be coming to get you, so we should get these drips out of your arm and make sure you are dressed and ready to go.'

'But Doctor,' I said quietly. 'What about paying for the hospital?'

'Don't worry, my child. All has been taken care of.' He winked at me and that just made me even more confused. Did the Bakers pay? Or Wasim? Or had no one paid and this was a public hospital? I thought it was best not to ask too many questions on this topic, so it would not backfire.

As the nurses removed my IV drip and fixed my bandages one last time, I realised I didn't have any clothes other than the hospital gown. I secretly wished that Maricar would come by with a bag of clothes. I was about to tell the nurse about my fashion issue when Maricar opened the door and walked in. Could this be the most serendipitous coincidence ever?

'Aubrey, Aubrey!' she shouted in excitement. 'You look so much better. Are you ready for your new beginning?' She held my face, kissed me on the cheek, and put a plastic bag on my lap.

I opened the bag and found a t-shirt, a pair of jeans, a fluorescent pink bra with matching panties, and sandals. Those clothes clearly were not mine, especially the fluorescent pink underwear. I looked at Maricar, confused, and she said in a whisper, 'It is from your friend downstairs. I know everything. Count on me.'

If anyone could make me feel better, it was Maricar. She held my hand tightly and helped me stand up and go to the bathroom to change into my newly acquired clothes.

Maricar informed me that Wasim was downstairs waiting for me and so was Danda. She told me that Danda reached out to her last night and explained the situation. She assured me she would keep it all a secret and I trusted her to do so. It was good to know I wasn't alone in this faraway land. I changed and collected a small bag with medication from the nurses. They showed me how to apply the cream on my wounds, and when and how to take the tablets I still needed to take for a week. Maricar then looked at me and asked if I was ready.

'I've never been readier for a new adventure,' I answered with confidence.

We walked silently down the corridor and pressed the elevator button to go down.

'What is the plan, Aubrey?'

'I don't know. Let's see what Wasim has for me.'

The elevator ride was swift. When the door opened, I immediately saw Wasim, his fat belly stretching the buttons of his shirt and his sweaty armpits staining the already-punished fabric. I walked all the way up to him and as he didn't say anything, I volunteered a conversation.

'I am feeling much better now.'

I paused. He still said nothing. He looked upset and angry but didn't say a word. He was starting to turn to go to the parking lot as I volunteered again, 'The doctor said I shouldn't sign anything while I was on medication, but I am discharged now. I know you had some documents with you last time that you needed me to sign. I am so sorry for all that happened, Sir. I am ready to sign anything you want. Just please, don't send me home,' I begged him with puppy eyes.

His face lit up immediately, struck by the arrow of hope in some cunning plan he'd probably thought he had to throw away.

'Come, Aubrey. The documents are in the van,' he said, optimistic and with a smirk on his face.

We walked to the van, where he opened the driver's door and fetched a wrinkled envelope. He took several pieces of paper out and handled them to me. He then dug deeply into the glove compartment of the car, looking for a pen, but found none.

'Never mind. You can sign this once you are back in the accommodation.'

'No, no, no. We should get this out of the way right now,' I insisted, already running back to the hospital, pretending to go look for a pen. He ran after me, shouting, "Wait, wait!" but I ignored him. At the hospital's main reception desk, there was a waist-high counter with a metal pen attached to a base by a chain, so no one would steal it. And as if by a miracle, right next to the pen, there was a paper cup, filled with coffee. The man next to me was getting his parking ticket stamped and I assumed it was his coffee. I wasted no time in holding the pen and knocking the coffee all over my t-shirt. The man next to me jumped in surprise. At this moment, Wasim was walking through the main door and saw me covered in coffee and looked puzzled as to what had just happened. I immediately started to scream, saying the hot beverage was burning my skin, although not a single drop had fallen on the bandages on my arms. The woman behind the counter tried to calm me down and the man whose coffee I had spilt backed up, looking guilty.

I grabbed the documents with my right hand and ran as fast as I could to the back of the hospital, towards the toilets. As I turned the corner to go inside the toilet, I felt a hand holding my arm. It was Danda, who saw the entire show and ran after me. Oh, my! How happy I was to see her! She told me not to go inside the toilet, but to continue walking down the corridor and take the second door on the left. This way, Wasim would have thought I was in the toilet and we would be able to exit the hospital through the emergency department entrance. We walked in silence, not running so as not to draw attention, and crossed the entire left wing of the hospital, emerging at the ER. From there, we snuck out a side door used by ambulance personnel and within five minutes, we were on the main street waving for a taxi. It didn't take long for one to come by and we jumped inside, my hands shaking and my heart beating extremely fast, adrenaline pumping through my body. I looked incessantly through the windows, trying to see if Wasim was following us but luckily, I did not see him. I wished I'd had the chance to say goodbye to Maricar, but I was sure that since now I had the documents in hand, the Bakers would protect me.

Danda told the driver to take me to her home in the Satwa district and within fifteen minutes, we were arriving at her home, a small apartment shared by four other people. I took a shower, changed into another outfit from Danda, and came out into the living room, where two other women were watching a video in a small tablet screen.

'I think you should call Mr Baker and let him know what happened,' said Danda in a motherly voice. 'Ask them if you can go to their home today, as we cannot fit you in this tiny apartment. They promised to give you a job, so ask if you can move in today.'

I picked up the phone and dialled the number written on a loose piece of paper. When someone answered on the other side, my mouth opened but nothing came out. I was so nervous that my voice failed me. The person insisted, "Hello. Can you hear me?" I took a long breath and answered back, introducing myself and explaining what had happened. Madam Baker had a soft, warm voice and told me she would be on her way to get me. Less than an hour later, she came by in a big grey SUV, a baby sleeping in the car seat in the back. She greeted me with a handshake at first, and slowly moved into a hug. I felt welcomed and safe, hopeful for a new start.

# 16

# THE BEGINNING OF THE END

Madam Baker seemed nice and was extremely polite. She kept asking if I needed anything and made sure I had everything I needed: towels, bed linens, personal toiletries, and even a separate cabinet in the kitchen with some food I could eat anytime I wanted. All my clothes were left behind in the accommodation and I did not expect to get them within the next few days. Danda said she would pass by there over the weekend but she was not sure if she could convince the others to hand my stuff over. For the time being, I was wearing Danda's underwear and the uniform Madam Baker had given me.

The house was very big and extremely well-decorated. It looked like a perfect home in a magazine. It had 4 bedrooms and a separate maid's quarters, which I was going to divide with their existing maid, Helen, a chubby and smiley girl from Ethiopia. Her hair was braided neatly, and I couldn't help but notice her beautiful and perfect white teeth. She spoke very little English, enough to communicate but I suspected we wouldn't chitchat often. Helen had been with the family for over one year and it was her first assignment overseas as a domestic helper.

Because of my injuries, or maybe out of pity, Madam Baker split the work so that Helen would be taking care of the house, doing the cleaning and washing, and I would be looking after the baby and doing the ironing. It seemed to me that I had gotten the best end of the deal and Helen did not look pleased with this arrangement. Before my accident, she had just been made the nanny and given the new-born baby in the house. With my arrival, she was back to being a cleaner.

In the evening, Mr Baker arrived and asked to see me. He looked worried and appeared much older than Danda had described. His hair was more white than grey and the deep wrinkles on his forehead made him look angry and tired. He was indeed very tall, and his accent reminded me of a TV news presenter. He spoke fast; too fast! Madam Baker entered the living room halfway through one of his sentences, tapped him on the shoulder affectionately, and seeing my confused face, asked him to slow down and pause between the words. He grinned at her, his teeth yellow and crooked. I could not help but wonder why someone with so much money would have such horrible teeth. He started again, this time speaking slowly and clearly, checking to see if I was actually understanding him every now and then.

'Aubrey, we are happy to have you here,' he said, calmly. 'My lawyer told me that he will go to the police tomorrow and log a report for how you have been treated and what your employer was trying to do with you. This will add to the blackmailing complaints we already logged. Do you have the document they wanted you to sign?'

'Yes, Sir. I can go and get them in my room.' I stood up and went to my new bedroom to get the document. He looked at it for a while, shaking his head sporadically. In the end, he smiled a fake, yellow smile and told me everything would be all right. He explained to me that they would try to settle my issue out of courts, as he had already offered to pay all my hospital expenses and would now proceed with getting me discharged from my employer and hiring me. He said I would have to go to the police station with the lawyer for a formal statement the next day, but it would be a routine procedure and I should not worry. Every time he told me 'don't worry', a red flag came up in my mind. Why would he insist on saying 'don't worry, everything would be all right'? *Should* I be worried? I had no idea what was going on. For all I knew, I had abandoned my job and ran away. Or was I still on sick leave and had the freedom to sleep anywhere I wanted? The rules of employment were confusing to me; maybe the company threatened us and kept so much from us so that this kind of situation would never happen.

I tried not to ask questions, feeling embarrassed for not being more aware of my own situation. Sometimes I thought they were being nice to me only because they felt guilty and had let me be electrocuted in their own house. But I truly wanted to believe, especially after all I had been through, that there were nice and good people in this world.

Mr Baker told me that was all and wished me good night. I took that as a hint that I should go to my room and stay there until called upon.

I didn't sleep until about four in the morning, tossing and turning in my new bed. Helen snored a little, not enough to wake me from a deep sleep but certainly enough not to let me fall asleep in the first place. All the events kept coming back into my mind over and over again and I wished I had Maricar and Lu to talk to. With no phone, no money, no SIM card, and no documents, I felt like a prisoner, powerless and isolated.

The next morning, Madam Baker asked me to look after the baby for about an hour while she worked on her computer. It felt like a test, to see how I would perform alone with her.

The child was an adorable three-month-old girl, golden curls starting to form at the back of her neck. Her name was Cleo, and that reminded me of the goldfish from Pinocchio's story. She was a friendly and calm baby, her rosy cheeks round like strawberry ice cream scoops and she had eyelashes that seemed ridiculously long for a child. Our hour together passed by in a flash and I caught myself smiling constantly. Finally, happiness was entering my life.

Two weeks later, Mr Baker asked to see me again. He said he had great news and was holding a manila envelope full of papers inside. He told me that my debriefing with the layer and the police went very well and that my old employer was now being properly investigated by the police for blackmail. He also told me they had accepted my resignation papers and I was one step away from officially being the Bakers' employee, under their sponsorship. All I had to do was to take a plane to an island called Kish in Iran, so the immigration officers in the UAE would stamp my exit from the country. I would then hop on the next flight back to Dubai, about four hours later, and the immigration officers would welcome me on my new visa. After that, I would go for some standard medical tests and get my new identity card. He said all of this in a calm, straightforward manner, as if it was the most common thing in the world to do, hopping on and off planes in a strange country like Iran, on an island in the middle of nowhere. He assured me that all expenses would be covered by him and I should not worry. Here he was again, muttering 'don't worry'. I nodded my head, consenting, not sure if I should believe him.

 Mr Baker explained the terms of my contract with him, a salary of four hundred and ten dollars a month, with accommodation provided but no days off. He said if I wanted something, I could ask them, and they would either buy it for me or take me to get it and ensured me that I would have plenty of days out with the family. That was a confusing deal, as I was hoping to be able to go out on my own as I had before, to see my friends and have some fun. But how could I push back if the only way I would manage to stay in Dubai was through their sponsorship? It did not look like his terms were up for negotiation and once again, I consented with a nod.

 Baby Cleo started to cry, and Mr Baker went upstairs, picked her up, and brought her downstairs into the living room. He sat down, looked into her eyes, and started to make funny noises, to which she responded with a giggle. I caught myself smiling again and left the room with a happy feeling in my bones, holding onto it for as long as I could.

# SUMMER – 2010

# 17

# THE TRUTH PREVAILED

Six months had passed since I moved into the Bakers' home and all my fears had gone. They were nice and understanding and baby Cleo was adorable. She could crawl and stand up straight if I held her by the waist, but she could not stand by herself or walk yet. She had this funny way of crawling with one knee moving up and forward and the other one sliding in a half-sluglike, half-catlike movement. It was cute. Helen, on the other hand, had been mean and grumpy from the beginning. She accused me of taking her job and forcing her back into housework and she threatened to poison me. She came from Ethiopia and I had no idea what kind of voodoo magic they practiced over there, but I was sure she did not really mean it.

The work was significantly less than what I had done at the cleaning company and I spent most of my time with Cleo. She was such a nice baby, calm and playful, and I did not understand why people complained that children were hard work. I did everything for her and even slept with her baby monitor in my room in case she woke up at night, so I could go to her and not disturb the Madam. I secretly felt a deep love for her and fantasised that she was my daughter. I was sure I had a bond that not even her mother had with her, which was sad to say, but nice to feel.

My wounds were all healed and the few trips I had to make to the hospital for follow-ups were all paid by Mr Baker. The visa process was also very easy and my fears of going to Kish were unsubstantiated. I had heard of people going there for the exit/entrance visa and getting stuck there due to incorrect paperwork and ending up spending months with no place to stay or anything to eat, resorting to prostitution to survive. Luckily for me, the Bakers had everything neatly organised and I spent only two hours there, inside the airport, just waiting for the flight back. A driver took me to the airport in the morning and then collected me in the afternoon to take me home.

Life was very routine now and although I was grateful to have this new job, I also missed my friends dearly. Not having days off was hard and I relied on the driver to buy me some basic necessities and top up my phone with credits. I went out with the family frequently, mostly to restaurants and shopping malls. The family was always generous with me and would invite me to sit at the table with them at restaurants and order some food.

Helen was getting increasingly jealous and started to sabotage my work, taking dirty nappies from the bin and placing them on the top of the baby changing unit, only to tell Madam I had forgotten to throw them away. She would spill milk on Cleo's bed and tell Madam I was being lazy and not changing the linen. Madam Baker confronted me a few times and even though I said I did not do it, I was not sure she believed me. At first, I doubted myself, but these accidents were happening more and more often, and I knew Helen was behind it. I became scared that Madam Baker would fire me, and I think that was exactly what Helen wanted. When I confronted her, she looked at me, and with an evil grin, she said, 'I was here first, and you took my job!'

My life grew more and more miserable, with Helen not only sabotaging my work but also poking holes in my clothes, undoing my bed linens, and even spoiling my food. Sometimes there would be too much salt or sugar or pepper in it. Whatever I left in the refrigerator in my designated containers, she would tamper with. I started only eating fresh food and not leaving anything in the fridge. Life was becoming hell again.

My luck changed one morning when, after Cleo had a bottle of milk, she threw up all over her pyjamas and I took her upstairs to change. Madam heard it and followed me upstairs. She took Cleo's temperature and changed her into a pretty green dress. As I was right next to Madam, I said I would take the dirty pyjamas downstairs to the laundry, which I did immediately, and came back upstairs to help with the baby. Cleo was fine. She might just have drunk the milk too fast, as no other sign of illness was present. I took her to the playroom and Madam followed me. We stayed there playing for about half an hour when Helen called for Madam, alarmed and with a horrified look on her face. Madam Baker thought something urgent had happened and ran after Helen into Cleo's bathroom.

'What happened, Helen?' asked Madam Baker.

'I have been telling you, Madam, that Aubrey is lazy and messy. Look at this!' Helen pointed to the sink, where Cleo's pyjamas were splattered everywhere, vomit bits dripping from the sink tap.

At this point, I was right behind Madam Baker, Cleo in my arms, quiet as an angel, looking at the commotion.

'How do you think this happened?' asked Madam Baker.

She knew exactly how it had happened. She saw me taking the pyjamas downstairs. This was going to be my revenge.

'I don't know how it happened, Madam, but this is Aubrey's job and she keeps on leaving Cloe's bathroom and room a mess. I am the one who always has to come and clean up. I don't trust her, and neither should you. She is not good for the baby. She is messy. She is not good, she… she…' Her words started to fail her when Madam's face showed no reaction to her complaints.

'If I were you,' Helen continued. 'I would fire her. I can do her job much better and you can have the cleaning company send someone for the deep cleaning.'

'Good idea, Helen,' Madam Baker said.

'Good idea?' I asked, perplexed and not believing my own ears.

'Yes, good idea,' Madam continued, 'because this is just what happened the other times, isn't it Helen? Like the time with the diapers, the food under the carpet, the pen marks on the walls, and even the breaking of Cleo's stroller, isn't it?'

'That's it, Madam. You see, she has been doing all of it. Why don't you just fire her?'

'So, Aubrey,' she told me calmly, 'please go to the play room and stay there with Cleo while I make a phone call. Helen, please clean this up and wait for me downstairs. I will have a better chat with you in a moment, more privately.'

I went to the play room, tears rolling down my cheeks. I hugged Cleo and tried to find comfort in her angelic face. Madam Baker followed me to the playroom and closed the door, something she never did before. The house had an open-door policy, and I immediately felt threatened. She asked to hold the baby and I handed Cleo over, sobbing uncontrollably.

'Aubrey, are you happy here?' she asked.

I could not answer, sadness blocking my throat. I wanted to say yes and no. I wanted to say that Helen was lying, but nothing came out. She came closer to me and looked into my eyes.

'All those stories from the last few months were lies from Helen, weren't they?'

'Y… Yes.'

'I suspected it and never took them too seriously. Today, I had the last evidence I needed. Please stop crying,' she begged me, sweetly. 'I want you to stay here upstairs with Cleo. Look after her. I will make arrangements to deal with Helen.'

And then she walked out of the room and closed the door behind her. Twenty seconds later, I could hear Madam outside the door, speaking on her phone.

'Michael! Thank God you answered straightaway,' she said, panicked. 'You won't believe what just happened!'

A pause followed.

'Don't tell me to calm down! I was calm until five seconds ago, I need to vent! Helen did her dirty trick again; this time, I saw it with my own eyes. And she was so insolent! She demanded that I fire Aubrey, ordering me about and lying through her teeth!'

She paused for about three or four minutes, just saying, "hm, hm" every now and then.

'Okay. I will call him now. Love you, honey.' She hung up, placing another call immediately. 'Hi, I need you to come to the house, please, right now. Thanks.' And she hung up again.

As she walked downstairs, I opened the door slightly, hoping to hear what would happen next. But she went into the kitchen and the house was too big for me to be able to hear anything. I sat there, playing with Cleo for at least an hour when Madam came, got Cleo, told me to go prepare the baby's food, and ordered me not to speak to Helen at all. I did not see Helen for the rest of the day.

At around six o'clock, Mr Baker walked through the front door, kissed his wife, and they both went into the living room.

'It is all prepared,' he said. 'Her flight is at eleven. Has she misbehaved?'

'No. I did as you told me. I sent her to her room, confiscated her mobile phone, and told the driver to stand by the door and not let her out. She cried a while and I think she knows what we are thinking.'

'Good. Let's go talk to her.'

They stood up and headed to Helen's room. They left the door open and I could hear everything from the kitchen, where I was feeding the baby.

'Helen,' Mr Baker said, his voice grave and oppressive. 'I want you to pack all your things right now. You have been disloyal and unprofessional. You lied to us. We know you are behind Aubrey's wrongdoings and today, it was the last straw. You are going home. Pack all your things. You leave in half an hour.'

Not a word came out of Helen's mouth. Shock? Panic? Anger? All I knew was that I did not want to be anywhere close to her. Maybe her threats would materialise into physical harm. Deep inside, I felt an enormous joy. Revenge had happened. The truth had prevailed.

Less than an hour later, Helen left the house, carrying two small suitcases, tears in her eyes. I did not feel sorry for her. She deserved it. She followed Mr Baker into the car, and the driver took them to the airport. I learned later that they had cancelled her visa immediately and although legally she could have stayed another thirty days in the country, Mr Baker had threatened to put a ban on her passport, so she would not be able to enter the country again. If she left now, she could return in the immediate future if she found another job. But I guess the Bakers did not want her hanging around the house for a month looking for a job, so they just bought the first airline ticket going back to Ethiopia and dispatched her. When I walked inside my bedroom, I realised Helen had left most of her things behind. Initially, I was afraid she would steal some of my stuff, not that I had much anyway. But looking around, I saw that her closet was still packed with things, from clothes and shoes, to kitchen items and an iron she had bought online and said she would ship to her mother. She clearly would not be able to pack everything she had in those small suitcases and I wondered what would happen to all the things she had left behind. I asked Madam Baker and she said, shrugging, 'Just put everything in these cardboard boxes. I will give it a month for someone to claim it; otherwise, we will donate it all."

That seemed fair. Helen had worked hard and saved money to buy these things. Even though I hated her, I thought at least a friend should come and pick it up to dispatch to her back in Ethiopia. One thing was certain: That person would not be me. I had no intention of helping her at all. And if I had learned one lesson, it was to continue to pray to God because He is listening and will come to help, eventually.

The next few weeks were delightful. I worked longer hours, but I was also happy to go to sleep at night and not have to worry about what my roommate would do to me, or have to lock my closet so she would not destroy my things. I cooked larger meals at lunchtime and just reheated them at night for dinner, without worrying that they would taste like vinegar. Life was pretty sweet.

# 18

# DREAMS OF FREEDOM

It was on a hot afternoon in June that Madam Baker asked me if I would be okay with travelling abroad with them over the summer. It was customary for them and most of the wealthy foreigners to leave the city during the super-hot months of summer. They all disappeared as soon as the school holidays started, and the Bakers would join the statistic of expat migration. This obviously only applied for the wealthy ones. Maids, drivers, and domestic helpers in general either got their annual thirty-days leave and went home to see their families or stayed behind looking after overindulged pets and manicured gardens. The luckier ones got to travel with their host families for the entire summer and thus, escaped the boiling weather in Dubai. To hit the jackpot meant going abroad to a European country or the United States. To be a nanny for a European family most certainly increased the chances of a big trip over the summer.

My answer to Madam was, of course, yes.

'To where, Madam?'

'A bit here and there,' she answered vaguely.

I looked at her with a puppy face and she thought for a moment before answering me.

'We will go to the UK. First to London, then to Bedford, and then to visit some relatives in Sheffield and Chesterfield. We might come back to London and then…'

She stopped halfway through her sentence, looked at me and began again, 'We will go to England. Travelling around.'

We both smiled. She did it out of politeness for the confusion. I smiled out of happiness to be going to England.

'How long will we stay? When will we go?'

'We will stay the whole summer. We leave Dubai on June twenty-eighth. I will need your help preparing everything for the trip.'

'Yes, Madam,' I replied, with a smile so big it showed my missing tooth at the back.

I was the luckiest girl in town. Not only I was going to Europe, but I would actually be landing in England. I wished I could see Maricar and Mariann's faces when I told them. All the women in the compound would be amazed and so jealous. I definitely needed to tell Danda and thank her. If it was not for her, I would be back in the Philippines, looking after a sick relative or washing dishes in a restaurant. And here I was, going to England!

The following couple of weeks were engulfed in a dream of seeing the Queen, double-decker red buses, and perhaps bumping into Mr Bean. I knew it was ridiculous, but I was one of his fans. I grew up watching his movies and the lack of dialogue meant his acting worked in any country. Would I see men in suits, little cars driving on the wrong side of the road, and palaces everywhere?

It wasn't until I managed to speak to Danda that I realised the opportunity was bigger than I had imagined. Danda had become a good and close friend over the last few months. After she helped me get the job with the Baker family, I felt a great sense of gratitude and appreciation and made an effort to call her frequently. Danda never wanted anything in return for all the help she had given me. Maybe that was what a true friendship was all about. I couldn't say the same about the other women in my accommodation. Lu, Maricar, Mariann, Jenny, and Honorata sort of lost touch with me after the accident. I called them a few times, but their answer was unanimously, 'I am too busy to talk now.' I became suspicious that maybe Wasim had told them not to contact me. Or worse, maybe he had threatened them. Week after week, we lost touch and after some time, I felt I could not call them anymore. Despite Helen's nightmare experience, I only had good things to say about my new job, and that would make them very jealous. Not having days off did not help, and my relationships deteriorated. Danda became my sole friend and confidant, and loneliness grew inside me. Baby Cleo comforted my heart with the knowledge that I was taking care of someone and having an impact on someone's life. Danda certainly had an impact on my life since the accident, and she did again when I told her on the phone about my impending trip.

'You are so lucky, Aubrey!' she announced overexcitedly, on the other end of the phone.

'I know, I will see all the touristic sites and escape the Dubai heat over the summer.'

'No, no, no! That is not what I meant. Of course, sightseeing must be nice, but don't you see what an amazing chance you are getting? You can just live there forever!' This time, I could hear her voice changing, almost in disbelief of my naivety.

'What do you mean?'

'I mean, you can live there. The salaries are so much better than here. Probably like ten times more. The working hours are ridiculously short, and you will be in London! The capital of the world!'

That last sentence scared me a bit. I knew Danda tended to have these Machiavellian plans and she was very street-smart, but her excitement was something I had never seen before. I could sense her jumping up and down on the other side of the line, smiling. My heart started to beat faster, and I was inundated by the same feeling of strength as when I forgave Lu in the darkness of my bedroom.

'This is so exciting, Danda! But how will I get a work permit? Where will I live? And I don't think Mr Baker will be too happy to see me go now, after everything he invested in me: the hospital bills, my visa, and all.'

'You never stop amazing me, Aubrey! Listen, you are not going to tell them anything. I know of a few people who went there and stayed. This is how it happens; listen carefully. Firstly, your sponsors will have to apply for a visa for you to go to the United Kingdom. Do you know if they applied for it yet?'

'Yes, they did. They asked me for my passport last week and I had to get some pictures taken also.'

'You are a lucky girl! They let you keep your passport? Most employers don't. Well, this is very good news. So, as soon as your visa is done, and your passport is returned to you, make sure to keep it safe. When travelling, if they ask for your passport, try to get it back as soon as possible. This will make your life less complicated afterwards. In the meantime, I will put you in contact with some people I know who can help you when you get to London. You can stay illegally over there and the chances of anyone catching you are minimal. You are not obliged to carry any identification with you while on the streets and you can always say, if asked, that you have a work permit. If you stay out of trouble, you can live there for years and years. Most people hire cleaners on an hourly basis and no one ever asks for a work permit. So long as you have some identification, you are fine. Take all your documents from the Philippines with you. In fact, if you decide to do this, take everything you can with you. You will not come back to Dubai ever again. Your sponsor will most likely put a ban on you, meaning you cannot return here. Once in the United Kingdom, you can live off part-time jobs here and there and you will save a fortune. My contacts can help you with accommodation in shared council homes, which are very cheap.'

'What are council homes?'

'You know,' she said in a condescending way, 'the government there gives free homes to poor people. Many rent extra rooms, and some move out completely and rent the place to people like you. All under-the-table arrangements, if you know what I mean.'

I didn't answer her, and we had a silent moment in which neither of us spoke for a few seconds.

'Aubrey, are you still there?'

'Yes, I am. I am just overwhelmed by all this information. Do you think I can really pull it off?'

'This is an opportunity you cannot miss. Do you know how many people would pay thousands of dirhams to be in your place? I can tell you twenty names right now of people who would risk their life just to cross the border into the United Kingdom. Think of all the migrants who get smuggled in trucks and ships over there. Many die on the journey. You are entering through the front door, airplane ticket paid for, hotel reservations made, and a clean tourist visa engraved on your passport. What else do you want?'

'I am sorry, Danda. I really want to do it. It is just that this is a lot to process and it does not seem fair to the Bakers and …'

She stopped me mid-sentence, shouting into the phone.

'Listen, this is your life! Over the last few months, you have been telling me that you have learned your lesson, that you will not let people use and abuse you, and that you have been waiting for your opportunity to make a move for yourself. This might be it!'

'You are right, Danda. I don't want to stay in Dubai anymore, risk not having my visa renewed when it expires, and then be sent home and spend the next twenty years dreaming of getting a job in Europe.' I paused, catching my breath, my pulse racing. 'Danda… I am moving to England!'

'Bravo!' she shouted and hung up the phone.

My hands were shaking, and I did not want the feeling of courage to ever leave me again.

Two days had passed when Madam showed me the visa in my passport.

'Congratulations!' she said, smiling warmly. 'Now all you need to do is pack your bags. We leave next Wednesday.'

It was a Friday morning and that announcement took me by surprise. For the last two days, I had not slept, thinking of all the things Danda had said to me. I thought I would have a few weeks until I could make up my mind, but with only five days to go until we got on a plane to London, I found myself pressured beyond belief.

After lunch, while Cleo was taking a nap, I went to my room and lit a candle for Saint Ignatius. Madam had forbidden me to light candles, as she said it was a fire hazard in her house, but this was an emergency. I needed all the help I could get and a candle and a prayer to the saint of decisionmakers seemed like the right thing to do. I got down on my knees over a folded towel on the floor and started to pray.

'Saint Ignatius of Loyola, intercede for me. You know that I have made a decision which is going to affect my whole life. Help me in the right way. Grant me your guidance and help me with what I want to do. And please, make my luck and my faith in my Lord increase every day. Amen.'

I blew out the candle and stood up. As I reached for the doorknob to open the door, my mobile phone rang. It was Danda! *Oh Lord*, I thought. *Could this be Your intervention? Already?*

'Hello,' I said nervously.

'Hi, my friend,' Danda said sweetly. 'How are you?'

'I am all right. Nervous, excited, anxious... but all right. I am glad you called. I needed to talk to you. It looks like I will be travelling this Wednesday.'

'Are you still thinking about running away?'

'I definitely am!' I said with confidence. 'You can be proud of me, Danda.'

I could not believe my own words. Anyone who knew me from a few months ago would not believe how self-assured I sounded. Adrenaline was pumping in my body; my mind was racing with so many questions for Danda.

'I need your help,' I told her. 'How do I leave them? When? Who do I contact there? What should I bring? What do I do with my things here? Madam told me I should only take a small carry-on bag with some clothes.'

'Calm down, Aubrey. I am glad you are excited to go. Are you absolutely sure this is what you want?'

'This is me taking control of the reins.'

'All right! You go, girl!' she sounded as excited as I was. 'So, here is what you need to do. Pack as much as you can, take all that is valuable with you. Take all your documents. Anything left that you cannot take, give to someone here before you go. I will be happy to take anything from you!' Her voice was giggly, and I knew she meant taking some of her own things back. 'Put it all in plastic bags and we can agree on a time when I can pass by to collect them.'

'No need, Danda. The driver can drop it off. I will tell him it is a shipment to the Philippines and he can drop it at your house in Satwa.'

'That's perfect. Thanks!'

'Then what?' I asked impatiently.

'Before you go, you need to reach out to Danilyn, my friend in London. I can give you her number. Send her a message saying you are my friend and explaining the situation. She will tell you what to do there once you run away. Also, take all the money you have. Ask your Madam for an advance salary, saying you want to send some money home before travelling, as you do not know how to send money in the United Kingdom. If she can give you two months' salary in advance, even better. Then, act normally, as if you are just joining them on their holidays. When you have an opportunity, you disappear. It's that easy!'

'I am scared.'

"I know. I would be, too. But if there is one person that can pull this off, it's you, my friend,' she said confidently.

We said our goodbyes and hung up the phone. About ten minutes later, baby Cleo started to cry, and I went upstairs to change her and get the afternoon schedule going.

# 19

# GONE

Wednesday morning arrived, and we left for the airport. The days before were hectic, getting the family's things ready for the trip, and the amount of stuff they needed for a child was incredible. Strollers, bottles, toys, and so many clothes. Baby Cleo had two large suitcases with only her things inside them. Suddenly, it felt unfair to have all my things packed in a small roller bag.

On Monday, the driver took a large cardboard box to Danda with the excuse of it being a shipment of presents to my family. He didn't ask any questions and as far as I could tell, Madam didn't even know he took the box. It was just another errand he ran.

Danda called me on Tuesday night to check if Danilyn had been helpful and to wish me good luck. Danilyn, Danda's contact in London, had told me of a place to live on zone 5 in East London, a short bus ride to the main touristic attractions in town. She walked me through the maths with salary, rent, and expenses, and said she had a client waiting list for house cleaning. She would recommend me and take a fifty percent commission on my payment. It seemed like a lot to me, but she was not prepared to negotiate. Danda said I could find my own clients and get the full payment for myself in a few weeks, so sticking with Danilyn felt like a good starting plan. She told me to study the city map and make sure I knew where we were going to be staying while there. She also gave me a couple of phone numbers in case I got into trouble and needed a lawyer or an escape plan. Under no circumstances should I mention her name to the police or any other authority. Danilyn had been in London for almost twenty years and sounded like the ring leader of a Filipino cleaning mafia. She was knowledgeable and precise with her instructions; a woman of few words who, at the end of one message, wrote me: *Find an English man and get him to marry you. That's the golden ticket!* I was not sure if she was married to an Englishman. In fact, I did not know if she was married at all, but her advice stuck with me. Maybe I would find love there. That would be the cherry on top of my adventures.

We left the house on time on Wednesday and I was told that my sole job was to care for baby Cleo. After we checked in, we went to the business lounge, a beautiful area with expensive-looking sofas, where enormous quantities of food were available for free and one could even get magazines to read without paying. I felt very out of place and uncomfortable. Mr Baker travelled a lot for his work and seemed to know the place like the back of his hand.

'Use these facilities if you need to change Cleo,' he said when we passed in front of some toilets.

I said I thought it would be a good idea to change her now, before we boarded the plane, and took Cleo inside while he and Madam headed for the dining area. The restroom had free nappies and wet wipes for the babies, and in the main area, it had free toothbrushes and toothpastes wrapped individually. I saw a woman finish brushing her teeth and throw the toothbrush away in the bin. What a waste! A brand-new toothbrush! The toothpaste tube was of a decent size and would last me two weeks at least. I discreetly collected three of each and stashed them inside my purse. The towels were cloth, not the usual paper ones, rolled one by one and stacked over each other like a pyramid. I wished I could take some, too, but there was no room in my bags. And I had to remind myself that soon, I would have to escape with only what I could carry, so less was more.

I left the restrooms and joined the rest of the family in the breakfast area. Food was plentiful, and Madam instructed me to eat whatever I wanted, but to make sure I had plenty, as I would have to look after Cleo on the plane.

At the time of boarding, an elegant woman in a beige-and-red uniform came to escort us to the gate, beautiful red lipstick making her lips pop with colour. At the gate, our passports were checked, and we walked down the corridor for a few meters when Madam told me that she and Mr Baker would travel in the front of the plane in business class and I would be staying with baby Cleo in the back. If there was an emergency, I should go get her or ask a flight attendant to notify her. She handed me the child and while she and Mr Baker entered a corridor leading to the front of the plane, I continued down into a second corridor which boarded the middle of the plane. At this stage, I was carrying Cleo, her enormous carry-on bag, and my purse, stuffed with toothbrushes and cupcakes from the lounge. The helpful attendant that once was all smiles was nowhere to be seen. I found my seat, strapped Cleo to my lap, and sooner than I expected, we took off.

The flight to London was a long one, almost the same length as the flight from the Philippines. I had forgotten all about that horrible trip almost three years ago, flying for the first time to Dubai. After landing, Madam and Mr Baker were waiting for us at the gate and we headed to immigration as a group. The three of them went on a separate queue for British nationals, while I stood in a very long queue for foreigners. The queue moved slowly, and I could see Mr Baker waiting for me on the other side. I started to get nervous, imagining scenarios in which the man at the counter would ask me too many questions or not accept my visa. All these worries were unfounded. When my turn came, the man at the counter was smiling and greeted me politely. He checked my passport and asked no questions. He handed the document over to me and wished me a nice holiday. What a great start in this country! I could already sense the politeness and friendliness of its people.

We got our luggage from the bag carousel and entered a car, which drove us all the way into the heart to the city. I stared through the windows, admiring the green landscape and the grey sky.

It took us almost an hour to arrive at our accommodation in London. It was a small apartment in an old building, and Madam called it an apart-hotel. It had two bedrooms, a small living area, a kitchen, a full bathroom, and a separate toilet area. I thought this was very strange, as the toilet cubicle had no sink next to it and it was on the opposite side of the other bathroom, which had a toilet, sink, and bathtub. The toilets also did not have the usual shattaf hand shower we got in all the toilets in Dubai. The arrangement was that I would sleep in the same bedroom as Cleo and Mr and Mrs Baker would be in the other bedroom. All the rooms were extremely small compared to the ones in Dubai and despite the building being very old-looking on the outside, the apartment was modern. The entrance of the Arlington House building had a large, brass front door and a restaurant next door, which I was told was very posh. A few steps through the door was the reception desk with a garden right behind it. I asked Madam if I was allowed to take baby Cleo there to play.

'Don't be silly, Aubrey,' she said, laughing. 'We are right next to a lovely park; the Green Park. We will go out there soon and in the coming days, if I am not with you, you can take Cleo there for a play and some fresh air.'

About an hour later, after I had unpacked our things, I placed Cleo on her stroller and we went for a walk around town. Just getting onto the streets was amazing. They were packed with short buildings no more than a few floors high, old-looking but well-preserved. The streets were tiny, and the sky was grey, but no real clouds could be seen. There were none of the skyscrapers or the dusty sky from Dubai. We walked a few meters down the road and Madam pointed to a corner building, where a man wearing a tuxedo and a top hat stood at the door. That was the Ritz, she said, and although I had no idea what 'the Ritz' meant, I shook my head and smiled. We walked a few more metres on a busy street and entered a huge park with green everywhere and the most beautiful trees I had ever seen. There were pathways in different directions and people were laying down on the grass having a picnic. We walked the length of the park and at the end of it, there was a magnificent square with white statues all around and a golden angel at the top. At the back, I could see a palace with soldiers dressed in red jackets and tall fur hats standing by the gate.

'That is Buckingham Palace,' Madam said. 'That is where the Queen lives. That over there is St. James Park, and this is a statue of Queen Victoria.'

Standing there, my mouth open in awe, I felt happiness and excitement, curiosity and amazement. Mostly, I felt like I had made the right decision to come and stay in this place. It was amazingly beautiful. I mentally thanked Saint Ignatius while Madam continued her tour-guide session. We walked past the gates of the palace and took Cleo to the playground at the corner of the park. We spent half an hour there and then walked along the lake, feeding the ducks. We saw squirrels climbing trees and sat down for a snack on the grass. I was in heaven.

The next three days were more of the same. We would go out with Madam all around town, sightseeing and having fun. The weather cleared up and amazing blue skies with fluffy white clouds formed above, and that became a magnet for people to come out and spend time on the streets. The place was buzzing with excitement. We went to several museums and I was shocked to find out they were free to enter.

It was while at the Natural History Museum that I got a message from Danilyn. I had written to her when I arrived in London but had not heard from her. In her message, she told me she would be free the next day and that I should make arrangement to leave tomorrow. She would meet me and take me to my accommodation and hook me up with some people she knew. Shivers went down my spine. My hands got cold and sweaty. I typed on my phone with shaking fingers, asking her how I could do it, as Madam was always with me. Her answer was brief: *That is your problem.* Her next message was: *Meet me at 14:00. Outside Arnos Grove tube station. At the carpark on the righthand side.*

I had to think fast and find a way to get some local money, find out where Arnos Grove was, pack my things, and escape Madam. I spent the rest of the day in a daze of anxiety. We went back to the apartment for Cleo's afternoon nap and I told Madam I had a bit of a headache and asked if I could lay down in a dark room for just a bit, so it would go away.

'Of course, Aubrey. Do you need some medicine? How bad is it?'

'Not too bad, Madam. Thanks. I had some Panadol with me and I took it already. I just need to wait a bit, so the medication starts to work.'

'Okay. Lay down and get better.'

I spent the next twenty minutes frantically using the wi-fi on my phone, searching for the location of Arnos Grove, which luckily was on the blue metro line that passed by close to the apartment where I was staying. That meant I could walk to the Green Park metro station and then take the metro straight there. I reckoned it would take me an hour to reach the place. I still had not figured out how to get some local money, but maybe I could exchange some dirhams on the way to the metro. That meant I should escape no later than noon tomorrow. But what if Madam decided to go out at that time? What if she didn't and we were just hanging around the house? How could I walk out? Fear took over and tears rolled down my cheeks.

Cleo woke up not too long after I excused myself. I picked her up, changed her nappies, and brought her into the living room to her mother.

'Oh, Aubrey, your headache must be really strong. Your eyes are full of tears!' She said worryingly and reaching out for some pills in her purse. 'Take these. They will make it go away.'

'Thanks,' I said shyly, wiping my cheeks.

'I have something to ask you,' Madam said, kindly. Tomorrow morning, I will go do some shopping and I want you to look after Cleo by yourself. Do you think you can do it?'

I nodded my head in affirmation.

'You can take her to Green Park,' she continued, 'and play in the grass. You can bring her home at around eleven-thirty for her lunch. I will be back shortly after that.'

That was the best news ever. What a coincidence! I'd never been too religious, but this was too much good luck at once. Saint Ignatius had become my hero!

I told Madam that it would not be a problem and that she should enjoy her free morning. I excused myself for a minute, entered the toilet, and closed the door behind me. I started a new message to Danilyn: *Madam is going out tomorrow. Just me and baby. Will find a way to escape.*

Immediately came a response from Danilyn: *Lucky. The customary approach is to leave the child in the stroller with a note with her name and a telephone number on it.*

Customary approach? How many people had done this before? Or was that just Danilyn's enigmatic way of saying things?

I opened the toilet door and took Cleo in my arms, afraid of what I would have to do to her.

The rest of the day passed smoothly. We met some of Madam's friends for an afternoon tea at a posh restaurant not far from the apartment. I did not get to taste any of it. The ladies sat there chatting, while I looked after the baby in the corner of the restaurant, under grumpy glances from the waiters. Bedtime was as routine as ever and after the lights were off, I packed my things in the roller bag and wrote the note I would leave the next day.

It took me four attempts to get it right. In the first one, I apologised to the Bakers, but I felt this was not appropriate, as the note on the stroller would be found by someone else. In the second and third attempts, I explained why I did it, but I ran out of paper. They were too long. The final piece looked like this: *If you find this child, call Mrs Zoe Baker - 07767374833*

I folded the three draft notes and placed them at the bottom of my bag. The final one I put in my purse. Then I went to sleep, my eyes heavy, my mind shutting down at once.

The next morning, we all had our breakfast in the apartment and at about nine o'clock, Madam left. She had instructed me to go to Green Park for a few hours but to return immediately if it started to rain, as the forecast predicted heavy rain for most of the day. The skies were grey but it was not raining yet. As soon as Madam closed the door behind her, I rushed to my room and collected my suitcase. I put the last few things I needed inside it and closed the zipper. Then, I got a few essential things for Cleo, put her shoes on, and left for the park. At the reception desk, the fat receptionist looked at me suspiciously, maybe because I was carrying a suitcase. I was about to go through the brass-and-glass door and he shouted, 'Excuse me!'

I looked back, and he was waving for me to come his way.

'I don't mean to intrude, Madam, but it seems that you have forgotten something.'

He pointed to my feet and, just then, I noticed I was not wearing any shoes. Embarrassed and trying to pull the legs of my trousers down to cover my white-and-red socks, I headed back to the elevator and then back to the apartment to get properly dressed. How absentminded I was, to forget my own shoes! My head was spinning, and I kept saying to myself, "Don't leave anything behind, don't leave anything behind!"

We left again and made our way to the park. The man at the reception desk giggled when he saw me but waved goodbye this time. We made it to the park and I had to find a good place to leave baby Cleo. We walked around a little bit, and everywhere, there were tourists walking or sitting on the grass. I found a quiet corner towards the end of the park, and as I took the note out to attach it to the top of the stroller, a drop of rain fell on my nose. And then another. Quickly, the sky turned dark grey and heavy rain started to pour down. I could not leave baby Cleo like this. The rain soon would get into her stroller and she would get wet and probably sick. It occurred to me that maybe she could get out of the stroller, crawl into the street, and get run over by a car! Or maybe a stranger would kidnap her! My clothes were all wet, my heart was pounding with nervousness, and my hands were shaking uncontrollably. I could not do this to Cleo. Deep inside me, I knew I loved her and I could not do this to her. I ran back to the apartment with difficulty, trying to keep the stroller straight while pulling the roller bag and moving in my soggy clothes. As I entered the building doors, the fat man from the reception desk greeted me with a 'good morning' and said sarcastically, 'I can see today is not your lucky day!'

What did he know? His comment sent shivers down my spine, doubt casting over my mind. *Maybe I should not run away,* I thought. But then I repeated to myself: *You can do it! You can do it!* I opened the door of the apartment, unloaded the stroller, and went to the bedroom to change. I put all my wet clothes inside a plastic bag and inside the suitcase. Then I went back to the living area and looked at Cleo.

'Why do I have to love you so much? It is almost eleven o'clock now. Your mom will be home soon. I lost my chance!'

I knew she could not understand me, but she crawled towards me and hugged me. She then crawled back to her playmat and picked up a toy phone. A lightbulb went on inside my head. My plan had to change. I went back to the bedroom, got my suitcase, and left it next to the door. I then put Cleo inside her crib with a few toys, kissed her forehead, went to the living room, and picked up the phone. I tried to dial Madam's phone number, but my hand was shaking too much, and I dialled the wrong number. I took a few deep breaths and tried again. This time, Madam answered.

'Hello,' she said happily on the other side of the line.

'Madam!' I said in a slightly panicked voice. 'Baby Cleo is crying too much. You need to come home.'

'What is wrong with her? Maybe she is just hungry?' Madam asked, slightly worried now.

'Just come home, Madam.'

I hung up the phone and rushed to the door. I knew Madam would rush back, and the last thing I wanted was to bump into her. I blew a sweet kiss to Cleo and left the apartment. As I headed to the elevators, I heard the telephone in the apartment ringing. Then it stopped. Then it rang again. I knew it was Madam calling back, trying to find out what was wrong. I entered the elevator, pressed the ground floor button, and even after the doors closed, I could still hear the phone, probably ringing just inside my head.

I made an effort not to run past the reception desk and just as I was about to exit the building, the man at the reception desk called for me.

'Madam!'

Why did he insist on calling me Madam? I was not a Madam! Why was he calling me? Did my Madam call him, as I was not picking up the phone upstairs?

I mustered all the courage I had in me and looked at him.

'Have a good day,' he said with a heavy English accent. 'No, in fact, *don't* have a good day. Have a *great* day!' He was smiling and bowed his head as a sign of respect.

I walked for the last time through the brass-framed door, disappearing onto the streets of London and moving towards my next life.

## THE END

# DISCLAIMER

This is a work of fiction. Names, characters, places, and incidents either are the products of the author's imagination or are used fictitiously. Any resemblance to actual persons, living or dead, businesses, companies, or events, is entirely coincidental.

Printed in Great Britain
by Amazon